*To the Bristol Writing Collective, for all the support and kindness —
especially Sylvia, who bought me a celebratory piece of cake when I
tentatively said, 'Huh. I think I've just finished writing my book.'*

1

DELILAH

I've always joked with people that I'm the evil twin.

I'm not evil though, I promise you. I don't have the moustache for it. But if you asked my father which of us would be the most likely to save the world and which would wreck it, Bea would definitely rock the hero role.

Not that I hold that against her.

Especially since she's currently out trying to save me from getting fired from my dream job after I made a *slight* wardrobe miscalculation and put myself in hospital.

Don't walk down steep stairs in new high heels, kids!

But don't panic. I'm okay. My ankle looks like a prize-winning turnip and my pride has taken a severe dent, but other than that, I'm good.

It does hurt, though.

A fact I'm desperately trying to hide from Jem – my sister's business partner and best friend from uni and the guy who can make my blood boil just by raising his condescending eyebrow in my direction.

Which he does a lot.

'You'll do yourself a mischief one day, making faces like that,' I mutter at the side of his head after just such an occurrence as he turns back from berating me for putting Bea out today to stare through the windscreen of the taxi he's come to collect me in from A & E.

I have to admit, I was shocked when he messaged to ask how I was doing earlier. He's the last person I thought would care. Except for maybe my dad. He's not exactly the nurturing type either. I'm much more likely to get a lecture from him about all the ways I'm going to mess my life up, unless I follow his advice to the nth degree.

Which of course I'm not going to do.

But I am going to prove to him I'm not the hot mess he takes me for. Even if it bloody kills me.

Jem – my other nemesis (is it possible to have two? Surely they're meant to be inimitable?) – is ignoring me now. It's his usual modus operandi around me, so I'm not entirely surprised by this.

Which is why I was blown away when he suggested he pick me up from the hospital after my X-ray. Though any warm feelings this brought about turned immediately tepid the moment I saw the expression on his face as he stomped into the waiting room to find me there with my leg propped on the seat opposite and a pair of crutches leaning jauntily against the wall beside me.

'Seriously, Dee, how do you manage to attract so much chaos?' he'd muttered, directing the first, but definitely not the last, eyebrow raise of the day at me.

'I don't need a lecture from you, Mr Living-By-Numbers,' thanks very much,' I'd quipped back, flashing him a serene smile.

'Maybe so, but I happen to have two working legs, so who's winning at life right now?' he'd pointed out.

I'd had to give him that. My ankle was killing me and I was

desperate to get out of the hospital with its migraine-inducing overhead lights and disinfectant-with-an-underlying-stench-of sweat smell.

'Why are you here, anyway, if it's such a major disruption for you?' I'd asked.

'Because Bea's going to be worrying about you, so I thought I'd help her out by making sure you didn't get yourself into any more trouble between leaving the hospital and getting back to her flat.'

'So, you're doing this for her then, not me?'

'Got it in one.'

Charming.

Which is actually a word I'd never use to describe Jem. He's the most uptight, po-faced—

'Thanks, mate,' I hear him say to the driver now as we pull up outside Bea's flat – which is currently doubling as her and Jem's office, as well as the place I'm going to be staying today, because there's a snowflake's chance in hell I'm getting up the steep stairs to my flat with my ankle in this state.

So there'll be no reprieve from his snarky presence for a while.

Jem gets out and, to my surprise, strides round to my side of the car and opens my door for me, holding out his hand in a helpful manner.

'How gentlemanly of you,' I say with a grin, putting out my own hand to be taken.

He doesn't return my smile and ignores my proffered digits. 'Pass me your crutches,' he says with a reproving expression on his face.

Huh.

I really don't need this attitude from him right now. I'm already feeling enough of an idiot as it is for hurting myself.

But I guess I'll have to suck it up. I'd be struggling to get out of the cab and onto my crutches on my own right now, after all.

So I slide them out from where they've been resting on the backseat and pass them to him, hoping my humiliation isn't showing on my toasty-warm face.

Why do these mishaps only ever seem to happen to me?

By the time I've levered myself out of the cab, he's got them propped up straight, ready for me to fit them under my arms.

'Thanks,' I say in my sunniest voice, determined not to let him know how much his disapproval is getting to me.

He just grunts.

I make my way, as quickly as my injury will allow, up to the Bath townhouse Bea's looking after for our dad while it's being turned into flats. She's living in the already converted garden flat, which thankfully only means climbing down one short flight of steps to the front door instead of up three precariously steep flights of stairs at my own place.

Turning to watch me hobble to the top of the steps, Jem holds his hand out again and this time, I just thrust my crutches towards him and lean against the wall for support while he takes them down to the front door.

On his return, he finally deigns to touch me by sliding his arm around my middle so I can lean on him and hop down the stone steps on one leg.

The moment we reach the bottom, he immediately releases me, as if it's horrifying to be close to my body, lets us in with his key, then strides off towards the kitchen.

'Want a cup of tea? I'm putting the kettle on,' he calls back to me.

Okay, so he can't be that pissed off if he's willing to make me a hot drink.

Look, I do recognise that he's probably a good guy, deep

down. If Bea likes him, then he has to be, I guess. She's a smart cookie and one of the kindest people I know. Too kind, maybe.

But it's the way he looks at me, like I'm something unsavoury he's stepped in, that turns him from hero to Captain Zero in my estimation.

'I'd love one,' I purr at him, determined not to let him see how much he bothers me.

Because he does bother me.

I've tried to be friendly whenever we've been around each other, but it's like he's determined not to like me, no matter what I do. I get that I'm not as serious a person as he and Bea are, but I'm not rude or unkind. Just a bit *unfocused* maybe. Clearly, this doesn't sit well with him and he lets me know it every chance he gets. At least it feels that way.

I've installed myself on Bea's king-sized bed, propping my back up against her pillows and my foot up on the cushions from her chaise longue, when Jem comes into the room, carrying a mug of tea. He puts it onto the bedside table next to me without a word and immediately turns to go.

'Jem?' I say, not entirely sure what I'm going to ask him, but experiencing a strong urge to delay him leaving me right away. I'm feeling a bit antsy now and I know for sure that boredom is going to set in quickly once I'm on my own.

'Yeah?'

'Uh. Thanks again for coming to get me. Seriously. It was kind of you.'

'Sure.'

'Can I... can I help you with anything today? To make up for the time you've lost?' I flash him a gracious smile, hoping he'll take it the right way.

'You can let me get back to work,' he shoots back, his voice flat and cool.

My insides squirm with humiliation. How does he always manage to make me feel like such a low-life?

'Fine,' I reply, matching his cool tone.

If that's the way he wants to play it, then so be it. I don't need his approval.

His returning nod is curt and he turns away and walks out of the room, closing the door firmly behind him.

Hmph.

Okay. I'll leave him alone and let him work then.

Alone, alone, alone.

I'll be fine here on my own. I've got my phone and a couple of books I can read on my reading app. Or I can watch a movie on the TV Bea has in here.

My thoughts slide to my sister and I wonder how she's getting on at my job. She's such a sweetheart to have agreed to step in and work there today – especially as it's meant she's had to pretend to be me in front of my boss – who hopefully won't be around much today, so won't notice the switcheroo. We're identical twins, but our personalities are about as different as you can get, so it's not a given that we'll get away with it.

And I know the subterfuge won't be sitting well with Bea. She's as straight as they come and always does everything by the book.

With any luck, the event we're running for my boss, Jonah's, best buddy will go smoothly today with Bea at the helm and any thoughts he's been entertaining about firing me will slip permanently from his mind.

I really hope so, because I can't afford to lose my job right now. It's a really well-paid role, which I'm totally unqualified for and was lucky to land.

I think the gods must have been looking down on me the day I interviewed for it because he hired me as his new marketing and events manager on the spot after only talking to me for a few minutes.

I suspect he was desperate to fill the position quickly.

I wasn't about to let on that I didn't know what the heck I was doing and that I'd fluffed up my CV with a few minor untruths (see Bea's CV for reference). I figured I'd work it out on the job. Trouble is, it turns out there's a lot more to know about that role than I imagined. But the way I see it, I spotted an opportunity and took it. These things don't fall into your lap every day, so when they do, you have to grab them with both hands.

Luckily, I have a brilliant sister who is very well qualified for it, even though she's chosen to set up a business with Jem instead of working for someone else.

Bloody Jem.

How can she stand to be around someone so uptight? I'd go crazy if I had to sit across from him and his condescending glare every day.

I stare at the door that he walked through twenty minutes ago.

He'll be plugged in to his computer, coding right now. Living the dream.

Some dream.

I can't imagine how stultifying it must be to sit at a desk, typing nonsense onto a screen all day.

At least I'm not doing that for a living.

Forcing my thoughts away from my sister's aggravating business partner, I try reading for a bit, but neither of the books I start grab me. Then I doom-scroll on social media for a while, but I can barely concentrate on the images flashing in front of my eyes and they all seem to blur into one. I lean back and sigh, tapping my fingers against my mobile, aware of my nerves pulsing under my skin.

My ankle is throbbing with pain and it's making it impossible to concentrate.

I'm not sure what to do with myself right now. I seem to have too much energy to sit still.

I take a sip of my lukewarm tea. Jem's made it with just the right amount of milk. At least that's one positive about him – he makes a decent cuppa.

I wonder what he's up to right now? I could actually be helpful if he'd let me. I could look through Bea's business emails and weed out the unimportant ones and alert Jem to anything that needs his immediate attention. Surely that would be useful? To have someone picking up the slack today?

And I can't just sit here.

Swinging my legs off the bed, I tentatively stand up, putting most of my weight onto my good foot. Yeah, I can easily make it from here to the office where Jem is without my crutches.

I'll just pop my head in and see if he can use me.

2

JEM

It's less than an hour after I've left her when Dee appears in the office.

No great surprise there.

I knew she wouldn't be able to stay in that room all by herself. She seems to thrive on other people's energy and will have been going slowly stir-crazy on her own.

From the moment I met her, she's rubbed me up the wrong way. There's just something about her attitude to life that gets my blood up. She may be an intelligent, attractive woman, like her sister, but she has none of Bea's emotional maturity and is very happy for other people to pick up the pieces she scatters around her as she bulldozers through life.

I can't stand selfishness, and she epitomises it. All she ever seems to do is take advantage of Bea's kindness and I'm sick of it.

I sigh and shoot her a resigned look as she inches into the room. 'Do you need something?' I ask, trying to hide my irritation.

She shrugs and gives me a cocky smile back, which I'm sure

works wonders on all the guys she charms on a day-to-day basis, but totally fails to have any impact on me.

'Just thought I'd stretch my legs. It's a bit tedious, sitting around in Bea's bedroom staring at the wall.'

'Well, I'm really busy and I need to concentrate, so can you stretch them somewhere else please.' I don't make it a question.

There's a short, tense pause. 'Yeah, sure. I just thought I'd see if I can help you with anything. I could check Bea's emails or something?' she says.

'No thanks. I've already done it.'

I continue to type. I just want her gone so I can focus on my work.

After a few more beats of silence, she asks, 'What's keeping you so busy today?'

'Programming.'

Another pause.

'What language do you programme in?'

I sigh and rub a hand over my eyes. So she's not leaving then. 'Python,' I say, my tone short.

'I'm sure there's a trouser-snake joke in there somewhere,' she says with a grin.

I shake my head, supressing a smile. 'Do me a favour and refrain from telling it.'

Her grin morphs into a frown and she huffs in frustration. 'Okay, Captain Code. I was just trying to lighten the mood.'

'I don't need light, I need peace,' I quip, turning back to stare at my screen.

But Dee is clearly determined to get the recognition she craves.

Limping over to me, she sits on the edge of my desk and rests her swollen foot on the arm of my spinny office chair.

I ignore the blatant play for attention.

'Are you sure I can't help with anything?' she asks, using what she obviously considers to be her most charming tone of voice.

My skin rushes with heat as her citrusy scent hits my nose.

'You can help by taking your foot off my chair,' I say, determinedly not looking at her as I try to get my perplexing reaction under control.

'I'm supposed to keep it elevated.'

'Yes, above your heart. You're not going to achieve that by sitting on my desk. You should go back to your room and lie on the bed with your leg propped up.'

I sense her scowling at the side of my head, but I don't react.

Clearly this doesn't sit well because she gives the arm of my chair a couple of gentle nudges in retaliation at my unfriendliness.

I continue to ignore her, pretending I'm not even feeling the jolts.

'I thought you'd brought me back here so you can play the hero and tell Bea you've looked after me while I'm in pain,' she says in a teasing tone. 'Contempt isn't a very heroic trait.'

Glancing at her now, I raise an incredulous eyebrow, then shake my head and look away again.

I think I can actually feel the irritation crackling in the air around her.

It may be a little childish, but I take a weird kind of satisfaction in it.

She's so easy to wind up because she hates not being the centre of attention all the time.

Bea thinks she acts this way because she says their father always treated Dee like she's second best and for some reason, she feels guilty about this.

I can't say I've ever seen any need for it, but what do I know? I'm an only child, so I've never experienced sibling rivalry.

Honestly, I think Dee's just a natural-born attention seeker.

My vision of the computer screen is momentarily blocked when she leans across the desk to pick up the empty mug next to me.

'Dee! For God's sake. I'm trying to bloody work here!' I snap before I can check myself. The disruption of having her in here has made me feel a little wired and my blood seems to be pumping at double its usual rate through my veins.

'Jeez, Jem. You don't need to be such a grouch,' she counters.

'You're like a bloody cat, trying to climb all over my keyboard for attention,' I say, aiming for levity.

'Are you implying I'm a nuisance?' she says with a sting of hurt in her voice, sliding off the desk and sucking in a sharp breath as her ankle appears to give her pain. 'Because I was actually about to go and make you a cup of tea. So there's no need to be unkind.'

I watch her limp away from me with my empty cup dangling from one finger, while she presses her other hand against the wall for support as she hobbles back to the door.

I experience a twinge of shame. Bea would not be happy with me if she could hear how short I was being with her sister when she's clearly in a lot of pain.

That's one of the things I love about Bea, her generosity and kindness. She's my ideal woman – not that I'd tell her that, not right now, anyway. It would make things too weird between us, especially as we're working together. But maybe one day…

There's a clattering sound from the kitchen, which drags me right out of my thoughts. What the hell is Dee doing in there?

Well, whatever it is, I'm going to let her get on with it while I get back to doing some work. There's still a lot of engineering to be done on this software before it's in a workable enough state to demonstrate to prospective customers – assuming we ever get through on a bid to pitch to them.

It's a risk, starting a business instead of getting a job with a firm right after university, but I prefer the idea of keeping control over the work I do, and I'll never get rich working for someone else. Unless I get really lucky.

After growing up in a household where we were always watching the pennies, I'd love to be in a position one day to be able to afford anything I want, without having to work out what I'd have to give up in order to have it.

It would also take a lot of stress off me if I felt confident that I could pay for my mum's ongoing and increasingly complex care needs in the assisted-living flat I've managed to get her into as well. We've already sold the family home my dad left her in his will in order to pay for it up till this point, but that money isn't going to last for much longer. It blew my mind to find out just how expensive care is for someone suffering with Alzheimer's.

The worry about how I'm going to pay for it is starting to keep me up at night and I was so tired this morning, I overslept and didn't even have time to shave.

Pushing away the heavy, sinking feeling in my chest, I focus back on the screen and resume typing for a few moments, but my concentration is shot.

Perhaps a break and a cup of tea would help.

If Dee really is making me one, she's going to need help carrying it back in here. I can't imagine she's going to be able to hop back to my desk without it splashing all over her.

I can imagine her trying it though, just to prove some kind of point, and the last thing I need right now is to have to take her back to A & E with burns.

Jumping up from my chair, I make for the door, but just as I swing it open and start to walk through the doorway, Dee appears right in front of me, heading back into the office.

As I predicted, she's carrying a cup of tea in one hand whilst using the other to steady herself against the wall. The surprise of my sudden appearance sets her off balance and she jerks away from me, shouting, 'Whoa!'

Unfortunately, this wild movement causes some of the hot tea in the mug to slosh over the rim and up into the air, then splatter down onto the front of my shirt.

There's a split second where I don't feel anything but the pressure of the liquid as it soaks the material against my skin, but the burning heat of it immediately follows and I let out a yelp of alarm. Tugging my shirt out from where it's tucked into my trousers, I yank it up and over my head before the tea has time to scald me too badly.

I'm vaguely aware of Dee hopping quickly away from me while I swipe any remaining liquid from my skin with the dry sleeve of my shirt.

Dee returns a few moments later and the next thing I know, I'm taking a glassful of liquid right to my face.

Too stunned for a second to react, I just stand there, agape, as the cold water runs off my chin and down my chest.

At least it's taking away any remaining sting from the hot tea.

Dee is also just standing there, frozen, clutching an empty glass in one hand, with her jaw hanging open and her eyes wide with what appears to be horror.

That's a new look for her.

'Shit! Jem, I'm so sorry. I wasn't expecting you to be there. You made me jump. Are you okay?'

'I've been better,' I mutter through clenched teeth.

She actually looks chastened and her gaze drops from my face to my chest.

A strange sort of gurgling sound emanates from her and her eyes seem to widen. 'I had no idea you were so fit,' she says in a strangled-sounding voice.

'Really? *That's* the comment you're going to make when you've just scalded me with hot tea?' I'm not sure why her compliment aggravates me so much, but it does.

Maybe because I suddenly feel exposed, standing here half-naked in front of her. I fold my arms across my chest, just below where my skin is still stinging a little from the burn. Looking down, I see it's only a bit pink and so a pretty minor injury, thank goodness.

'Sorry. I really *am* sorry. I didn't mean to make you feel uncomfortable about, you know, your body, on top of everything else,' she whispers.

Huh.

This is a totally different Dee to the cocky, self-centred one I'm used to seeing. When I look back into her eyes, I see with a shock that they've welled with tears.

'Hey, don't worry about it,' I say on reflex, giving a small shrug. I feel bad now for being so snappy.

There's an uncomfortable pause where she blinks hard, trying to clear the tears.

God, this is weird. And uncomfortable. My heartrate seems to have picked up again and I can feel my pulse throbbing in my throat.

'Important to exercise when you're sitting at a desk all day,' I say gruffly, to break the tense silence. 'I go climbing at the wall, so I need to be fit for that too.'

'Oh, right. Yeah. I guess so,' she says. 'Well, I didn't mean to get so personal. I think it was the shock that made me blurt out the first thing that came into my head.' Her gaze isn't meeting mine now.

She's embarrassed.

Another first.

'I didn't mean anything by it,' she says, still staring at my chest. 'It was just an observation. You're always wearing such baggy shirts so I've never really thought about your body before.'

There's another weird, tense pause while we both digest what she's just said.

'Um... er... anyway. Do you need anything to put on that burn?' she asks brightly now, apparently determined to pretend there's nothing strange going on here. 'A cold flannel or something?'

She's still not looking me in the eye and a strange kind of prickly shiver runs over my whole body.

What the hell?

'Er. No. I'm fine. The water you threw all over me did the job,' I say, trying to keep my own tone light now.

'Okay. Good.' Another awkward pause. 'Do you have another shirt to wear? Or should I put this one in the wash? Bea might have a big jumper you can borrow for a bit. I could look in her wardrobe.'

'Don't worry. I have my gym kit with me, so I've got a t-shirt I can put on.'

She just nods once, then starts to hobble back away from me. Finally looking me in the eye, she says, 'Well I'll leave you to it then. I'll stay in my room so you don't need to worry about me attacking you with any more tea.' She flashes me a smile now and I see the old mischievous Dee has returned.

Which I'm relieved about. I was feeling really odd about seeing her so unsure of herself.

She limps away without another word and I stare after her for a moment before going back into the office, pulling my gym t-shirt out of my bag and putting it on. The burn prickles a little as the material brushes my skin, but I ignore it.

I also ignore the squirming heat in my belly.

After making myself a fresh cup of tea, I sit back at my desk and stare at the screen with unseeing eyes until I finally manage to pull myself together and get back to work, pushing away a lingering, unsettled sort of feeling in my chest.

3

DELILAH

What the hell happened there?

It was the weirdest thing. The moment Jem whipped off his shirt, after I accidentally showered him with hot tea, my whole nervous system went into overdrive and I lost the ability to control my speech. I have no idea why the sight of him half naked fried my brain like it did, but I was suddenly reduced to the mental state of an inexperienced thirteen-year-old girl.

Not that having a hot bod makes Jem any less annoying. He's got a knack of knowing exactly how to cause me maximum pain and humiliation and he uses it to full effect whenever he can.

The guy's a pain in my butt.

Unfortunately, this thought only leads me to wonder what his butt looks like naked, which I really, really don't want to be thinking about right now. Not when I'm in this state.

He's annoying and frustrating and I absolutely *do not* care what he looks like naked.

I've no idea why I'm thinking about him like this. He's nothing like the cool, fun guys I usually date. He's totally not my type.

I lower myself carefully onto Bea's bed and prop my foot back up on the cushions, then lie down, making sure my swollen ankle is above my heart.

Bloody know-it-all Jem.

Pulling my phone out of my back pocket, which is difficult because I'm lying on it, I open one of my social apps and blindly scroll through it. To my annoyance, all I can see is the vision of Jem's honed chest and muscular arms in front of my eyes.

Grrr!

Why am I feeling like this? It must be a delayed reaction to the shock of hurting myself and having to go to hospital earlier. That has to be the explanation. That's why my heart is racing and my whole body feels hot and kind of fizzy, like there's static under my skin.

I need a distraction. If only Jem had given me something to do. I'm going to be so bored lying here on my own and I'm in too much pain to sleep.

I stare around the room, taking in the characteristic neatness of my sister's domain. Everything is in its place and scrupulously clean. It's the complete opposite of my own bedroom.

Ugh. How the hell am I going to get up all those stairs to my attic flat with one leg out of action? I wonder whether Bea would mind me crashing here for a couple of days, just till I'm a bit more mobile.

I'm sure she won't. She's a good un' like that. Always looking out for me.

Unlike my bloody parents.

In fact, I think landing the job at the hotel provoked the first compliment I can remember ever getting from my dad.

After a godawful row that I had with him over a restaurant dinner a while ago, he'd stopped my allowance, which was covering my living expenses while I was between jobs, till I 'grew up a bit', so being able to wave getting the events role in his face was satisfaction personified.

It was weird, and gratifying, to see a look of almost humbled approval on his face.

I actually went home and cried happy tears after seeing him, for once.

Which is why I can't lose this job now and why I begged Bea so hard to step in for me today. I don't want that one sweet memory of my father's admiration to be obliterated by his subsequent return to disappointment.

Hence all the subterfuge.

But it's all part of growing up, right? Becoming an adult? Learning how to turn opportunities to your advantage.

You have to have agency these days to get anywhere in life, as I've come to discover after struggling to hold on to a permanent position after graduating from art college.

You see, I'm actually an artist – at least an aspiring one. I've yet to make it to the big time and actually start to sell my art – so the opportunity to be in a position to persuade Jonah to hang some of my paintings in the hotel, where wealthy people are bound to see them, felt like a gift from the gods.

Another worrying thought suddenly occurs to me. How am I going to get around at the hotel all day tomorrow with my leg out of action? I can sometimes cover a lot of ground on a day-to-day basis as I move about the place doing my job. Jonah is not going to be happy with me if I'm not up to my usual speed – which, to be fair, isn't exactly speedy. But I've not been working there very long and I'm still winding up to top gear.

Hmm. No point in panicking right now though when there's nothing I can practically do about the situation. I need to find out how it went today first, anyway.

Maybe I should watch a movie to while away some time, just till Bea gets home.

* * *

I've watched one and a half movies and started the first episode of a new series before I hear Bea finally coming in through the front door to the flat.

I sit up against the pillows, wincing as pain shoots through my ankle when I shift it on the cushions. I'm desperate to hear how she's done at my work today, so I'm staring at the door in anticipation when she walks through it with a smile on her face and colour on her cheeks.

'So? How did it go? Did the event run okay?' I ask her, feeling tension twanging in my shoulders. If not, there's a good chance I'll be out of a job and back to square one with my life plan.

But of course, my practically perfect sister's not about to let that happen.

'It went really well,' she says breathlessly.

I relax in increments as she runs me through how brilliant she's been today.

Then she drops the bombshell that my boss is still thinking about firing me. He hates my marketing plan, or what I've been able to scrabble together of it so far, at least.

Ah, hell.

I guess I was kind of expecting it. I've not exactly been smashing it at work recently.

What I'm not expecting is for my sister to announce she's going to save my bacon by holding one of her friend's festivals at the hotel this coming weekend. And that she's happy to keep going in as me to make sure it runs okay.

'I just need to clear it with Jem, but otherwise I'm good for it,' she says, but I can see from the expression on her face that she's going to make sure he agrees, whether he wants to or not.

She's *excited* about doing it.

Huh.

I'm really surprised by this. I expected her to be desperate to get back to her business here with Jem, but it seems like she's actually fired up about getting the hotel back on its feet.

Which, I guess, is a great outcome for me.

'Okay then, let's go for it,' I say, ignoring a niggle of worry about how bored I'm going to be for the next few days, sitting alone here in her flat while I recover. Perhaps I can use her desk and work on the marketing plan while she's at the hotel.

If Jem doesn't lock me out of the office, that is.

There's a freaky squeezing sensation in my chest at the idea of being around him for the next few days. It's probably just irritation though, so I push all thoughts of him away. He's of no significance right now.

Unlike Jonah. I wonder whether he was in any way aware that he was around my sister today instead of me. It's unsettling to think we're so easily interchangeable. We're very different in so many ways, but then with only cursory attention paid, it would be easy to mix us up, I guess. Apart from us having different hair.

'So how did you get away with your new hairstyle?' I ask her, pointing at her long curtain of blonde hair that she's had since we were little. I, on the other hand, chopped mine into a sleek bob ages ago, via a few other hairstyles. Partly because I like to change up my appearance on a regular basis, but also to set me apart from my sister. We've grown more distant since we were little kids, but I've always needed to have my own identity, outside of being an identical twin. Especially since my counterpart is as shit-hot as Bea is.

Comparison breeds the *mother* of all insecurity.

'I'll need you to cut it off for me,' Bea states, to my utter amazement. It seems she's going all in with this ruse and is even prepared to change her appearance for it. While I'm grateful for her dedication to help me keep my job, I'm shocked that she's willing to do something so radical.

And, if I'm honest, I'm not entirely happy about her aping my style.

But who am I to complain right now? She's doing this for me, so my qualms need to shut the hell up.

So I say, 'Ok-ay. Grab the kitchen scissors and I'll chop it off for you.'

* * *

Which is why, when Jem pokes his head around Bea's bedroom door to let her know he's heading off home, we're sitting side by side, staring at ourselves in the mirror and marvelling at exactly how alike we look.

'Whoa!' he says, looking between us, then fixing his gaze on Bea. 'What happened to your hair?'

So, I guess there must still be something different enough about us if Jem can tell us apart on first glance.

I experience a swell of hurt as he completely ignores me to hold a conversation with Bea, as if I'm just her pale reflection.

Looking away from them, I stare down at the screen of my phone as they discuss business, relieved when Bea gets off the bed to go and conduct her conversation with him outside the room, so I don't have to studiously keep my eyes off his fit body under that fitted gym t-shirt, the naked image of which I now can't unsee. It's been burned onto my vision, like a ghostly echo after you've looked at something that's too bright.

As I predicted, when Bea comes back into the room, she

suggests I stay here in her flat and that she goes to stay in mine till my ankle's recovered enough to get up the steep, narrow stairs to my attic-level floor.

It's a no-brainer, of course. And the best thing all round for both of us – this room's not really big enough for two very *independent* sisters to share – so I make no attempt to protest. It would be useless, anyway. When my sister wants something, she bloody well gets it.

So that's that, then. I'm staying here for the next few days. In a flat with a man that makes my blood boil, coming and going as he pleases.

Well, I guess I'm just going to have to tough it out. And so is he.

I can't imagine he was too pleased to be told he'd be treated to my company all this week either.

Oh well. It's only for a finite amount of time.

What's the worst that could happen?

4

JEM

I come into work the next morning in a strange mood.

I'm not entirely sure how I'd describe the way I'm feeling today. Agitated, maybe. Disrupted, certainly. Nervous?

Hmm. Kind of.

Maybe it's because I'm not sure how it's going to play out having Dee in the house while I'm trying to work. She has a knack of getting in my face just as I'm finding a rhythm with something. At least, that's been my experience so far.

She's not been living in Bath for very long, but from the moment Bea introduced her to me, there's been something sort of spiky and *off* between us. I think it's because I find her overconfident, *look at me,* flirty-teasing attitude a bit difficult to navigate. It's virtually impossible to concentrate on anything else whenever she's in the room – like she sucks up all the energy to power herself, or something. I don't know. I can't quite explain it. I guess my lack of experience when it comes to relationships puts me at a disadvantage here. So I just try to ignore her, but this seems to make her even more determined to get my attention, for some reason.

It's all just a bit bloody *much*. Especially when I'm trying to work.

So I've decided the best thing is to give her a wide berth while she's staying in the flat. There's plenty of coding work for me to be getting on with while Bea and I wait to hear whether we've made it through the upcoming funding round to allow us to take the business to the next level.

This enforced hiatus is also why I said okay to Bea continuing to help Dee out by doing her job at the hotel this week. Not that she gave me a lot of choice. It was clear she'd already made up her mind she was going to do it. I figured it was fair enough for her to have a couple of days away from the start-up though, because she's been working so hard to get us into a position where we'll be able to hit the ground running when – and I seriously hope it's *when* – we get the money behind us that we need to turn it into a going concern.

After letting myself in through the front door to the flat, I'm relieved to find the place is quiet. There's no Delilah in the kitchen or the office and the door to the bedroom is firmly shut.

Good.

With any luck, she'll stay in there all day.

I make myself a cup of tea, trying not to think about the weirdness of yesterday when she'd thrown a cup of the stuff at me, then gone gaga when I'd taken my shirt off.

It's not like she's never seen a guy half naked before, I'm sure, but maybe her strange reaction was because it was me. The guy she thinks of as some asexual robot that she can't understand her sister's friendship with. Like a Ken doll with no sexual organs.

I'm just Jem.

Ugh. What the *hell's* wrong with me? Having Dee around seems to have scrambled my brain.

Unfortunately, even though it's my plan to stay well away

from her, it seems it's not hers and after only an hour and a half of sitting at my desk, I sense the door to the office open. I glance away from my screen to see Dee come hobbling into the room.

'Morning,' she says, her voice bright, as if nothing untoward happened yesterday.

Thankfully, she's dressed and her hair looks wet, as if she's recently got out of the shower and hasn't got around to drying it yet.

A rogue thought about how she managed in the shower with her damaged ankle leads to an image of her actually in the shower, and I swallow hard and experience an unwelcome flash of heat across my skin.

No.

I'm definitely not entertaining that thought.

She's an attractive woman, I'll admit that, but she's not my type. She's way too self-involved and needy.

'Morning,' I reply, looking straight back at my monitor. I don't want her to think it's okay to just stroll in here and interrupt me when I'm working.

There's a loaded pause where she hovers near the doorway, as if weighing up the wisdom of trying to talk to me again.

I ignore her.

She gives a low cough, then out of the corner of my eye, I watch her hobble further into the room.

'Mind if I use Bea's desk?' she asks. 'I've got a marketing plan to work on.'

I try not to sigh. It's going to be impossible to not be distracted by her presence in the room. The palpable aura of restless energy she always gives off makes me vibrate with tension.

But I can't exactly say no. It's Bea's flat and Bea's desk and she's invited her sister to stay here.

'Go for it,' I mutter, not wanting to sound too keen, in case she thinks I'll be up for chatting all morning.

'Thank you kindly,' she says, her tone level and reasonable, as if she's understood my tacit request to work quietly.

At least I hope that's what she's gleaned from it.

That hope lasts for about twenty minutes.

'Jem?'

'Huh?' I grunt, frustrated at having my concentration broken when I'm in the middle of writing a complex line of code.

'Can I borrow your phone?'

'What?' I finish what I've been typing and turn to look at her, not sure I heard her right.

'Your phone. Can I borrow it for a sec?'

'Why?' I ask, suspicious.

What's she up to?

'I want to take some photos of my ankle to send to a friend who's training as a physio. She wants to see what it looks like. I told her, hideous, but she's professionally fascinated.'

Her tone is light with amusement, but I'm getting the impression she's bored and trying to get me to play with her.

'I don't want photos of your feet on my phone, thanks very much,' I joke.

She throws up her hands and lets out a loud, exasperated-sounding sigh. 'Come on, Jem, don't be such a tight-arse. I only need it for a minute. I'll delete the pictures the second I've sent them to my email, I promise.' The grin she gives me is one of pure mischief, though.

A pulse starts beating in my throat.

'I thought you were working on your marketing plan,' I point out.

'I am. But I'm finding it hard to concentrate because of the pain in my ankle so I'm just taking a quick break,' she fires back.

I sit back in my chair and fold my arms, giving her a level stare.

She just stares right back at me.

The confidence on her is something to behold.

Clearly, she's not going to leave me alone until she's got what she wants. Typical Dee.

Something occurs to me. 'Hang on a second. Why can't you use your own mobile for taking photos?'

A pained frown crosses her face. 'Because when I twisted my ankle, I dropped it and it bounced down the stairs. It must have damaged the lens on the camera because it won't work any more.'

Hmm. Is she having me on? I wouldn't put it past her.

But I also don't have time for this kind of ridiculous argument. So I sigh, then pull out my phone from my back pocket and hold it out to her.

Getting up from Bea's desk, she hops over and takes it from me with a smile.

'Hang on,' I say, waving for her to give it back to me. There's no way I'm telling her my PIN. Holding it up to my face, I unlock it, open up the camera app, then hand it back. 'Be careful with it,' I warn her.

'Of course,' she says, one side of her mouth crooking into another mischievous smile as she hops back to the desk and sits down. I try not to watch her as she whips off her sock and rolls up the leg of her sweat pants, then starts taking photos of her ankle from all different angles. Dragging my gaze away, I stare back at the computer monitor, unable to focus on the text right in front of my face. Something's bothering me. But I'm not sure what. There's a niggle of concern at the back of my brain.

Glancing back over at her, I see her swiping at the screen of my mobile, then staring down at it in what looks like stunned fascination. Surely pictures of her ankle can't be that interesting.

She blinks a few times, then glances over at me, her eyes a little narrowed.

That does not bode well.

But I shrug off my worry. She's probably just messing with me again.

There's nothing incriminating on there.

Is there?

I don't even want to think about it.

And then I do. And I remember the photo I took the other day. And my blood runs cold.

'Er, Dee. A-actually, can you give it back,' I say haltingly, holding out my now shaking hand.

My blood is suddenly thundering through my veins and my face is radiating heat.

She gives me such a penetrating look, I know for sure she's seen what I really didn't want her to see.

'When did you take this photo of my sister?' she asks. 'And more to the point – why?'

'Just give it back,' I mutter, unable to think of a single good excuse for the picture I have of Bea on my phone.

I'm ashamed to say I took it without her knowing the other day, when the sunshine was pouring in through the large windows and highlighting her golden hair. She was leaning back in her office chair with her hands behind her head, staring off into the distance, with a small smile on her lips and her eyes shining with an expression of such warmth, I almost asked her what she was thinking about. But I didn't want to break the spell. She looked so ethereal, so beautiful, I just wanted to capture it so I could look at it properly again later and remember how it had made me feel, without seeming like a creep.

I know, I know, I should have asked her. But I was too embarrassed to. I didn't want to have to explain why I wanted it.

It's been such a long time since I experienced anything approaching peace, what with losing my dad a few years ago and being well on the road to losing Mum too, and right then, looking at Bea, spending quality time with her and being privileged enough to call her a friend, I actually felt a calming sort of contentment.

Like there could be happiness in my future.

Not that I'm about to say all that to Dee.

It's none of her business how I feel about her sister, or the state of my mind at the moment.

'I'll give it back if you tell me about this photo,' she states, raising both eyebrows in challenge.

'No deal,' I counter.

'Is this what you wank to?' she shoots back. The tone of her voice has changed; though it's still jokey, it's more brittle. Accusing, even.

'No. Give it back. Now.' I change my own tone to match hers and get up out of my seat, holding out my hand as I stride towards her, my heart pounding against my chest.

She gets up too and folds her arms, tucking my phone against her side.

This, it seems, is war.

'Dee, I'm serious,' I warn her.

'Yeah? Me too. No tell, no phone,' she counters.

Blood is now pounding hard in my temple.

'Give,' I state again.

'Are you in love with my sister?'

The question stops me in my tracks. It's so direct, so bold, I'm at a loss about how to reply.

I mean, I guess I am in love with Bea. Always have been. But I've never told her. Never acted like I am. She's never given the impression she feels like that about me and I've not wanted to damage my friendship with her.

I'm biding my time. Waiting for something more to develop naturally between us.

I feel sure it will eventually, given how much time we spend together on a day-to-day basis.

'It's just a photo,' I say, keeping any emotion out of my voice. I don't want to give myself away to Dee like this. She'll only use it against me, I'm sure of it.

'It looks like more than that to me,' she says. 'I'm an artist, don't forget. I see subtext in everything.'

The snort I let out sounds extra loud in the silent room.

'You wouldn't recognise subtext if it bit you on the arse,' I say, annoyed that my voice has taken on a bit of a shake now.

The corner of her mouth quirks. She's enjoying this. Thriving on the drama of it.

She takes a step towards me, taunting me with her eyes. She's looking for an emotional reaction.

But I'm not going to give it to her.

'Phone. Now,' I say again. 'Or I'll call your boss and tell him about this ridiculous ruse you've emotionally manipulated your sister into doing.'

'You wouldn't dare!' she says, her forehead creasing into a frown.

'Try me.'

We glare at each other, our gazes locked. We're like two big cats, poised and ready to tussle.

The air seems to crackle with tension between us.

Who will break first?

'Well, what's your next move?' I ask, my voice rough. I'm intensely aware of the heat that's radiating from both of us. Like our mutual animosity is transforming into kinetic energy.

My heart is still thumping hard and I see her swallow, then blink rapidly.

Aha! I win.

She confirms this by unfolding her arms and thrusting my phone towards me. 'Fine. Take it. But I know what you're all about, Jem. I see you. Don't forget that.' Her tone holds a warning, like she's telling me she'll protect her sister from me, no matter what it takes.

Yeah, well, we'll see.

And with that last retort, she turns on the spot, which clearly gives her a shooting pain in her ankle because she sucks in a sharp breath, before hobbling quickly out of the room, slamming the door behind her.

The sound of it rings in the air for a few moments and I run my hand over my tense face, wondering what the hell she's going to do with this new information that she thinks she has on me.

Okay, that she *does* have on me.

I dread to think.

* * *

I don't see her again for a few hours.

My concentration is shot for the day though, so all I can do is stare at the screen and type crap, then delete it and start again – *over* and *over* again.

At least her absence gives me time to calm down from my adrenalized high, so by the time she appears in the office again, right before I'm thinking about heading home, I'm in a much calmer state of mind.

She's not going to say anything to Bea, I've decided. If she tries to hurt me, she knows I'll hurt her right back.

And as long as I manage to come up with a good excuse for

why I had that photo of her, I'm sure Bea will brush off any suggestion of there being anything improper in my behaviour.

At least I hope she will.

Dammit. I wish I'd just deleted that picture. Or at least taken it out of my Photos app.

Anyway, it's done now. No point in getting stressed about something I can't change.

'Hello,' Dee says to me now as I shut down my computer and tidy my desk, ready to leave.

'Hi,' I say, not looking at her.

'I just came in to apologise,' she says.

I turn to look at her, confused.

'What?'

'I said I wanted to say sorry. For earlier. It wasn't cool.'

All I can do is stare at her. What's this all about? She can't actually be apologising. Can she?

'What do you say to *that*, Numbers?'

There's a strange lilt to her voice and it's making me nervous.

'Only you could use the word *numbers* as an insult,' I reply.

'Only *I* can do a lot of things you don't know about.'

I frown. What the hell's got into her? It's not unusual for her to be so posturing, but this is a whole other level of bravado. 'Are you okay? You're acting very strangely.'

'No. *You're* acting,' she shoots back at me with a slightly lopsided grin.

I snort in confusion. 'I'm really not.'

'Yes, you are. All of this is an act.' She walks over to where I'm standing by my desk and lifts a hand to pluck at the collar of my shirt. 'It's just a disguise you hide behind.'

I let out a huff of surprise. This is even weirder behaviour than before. Has she necked a bottle of vodka or something?

There's a strange, hazy look in her eyes that makes me think she's not altogether sober.

'And what am I supposed to be hiding?' I ask, my voice level.

'Your soft side.'

'My what?'

'I know you're probably a big softie when you let your guard down,' she says.

I roll my eyes and mutter, 'Christ.'

'Don't be embarrassed about earlier,' she teases. 'When you flashed your bod at me, I mean.'

Folding my arms, I stare at her. 'I'm not *embarrassed*. I am, however, freaked out by you right now.'

She ignores this and says, 'I tell you what. I'll show you mine, then we'll be even and you can relax around me again.' She gives me what I suspect she thinks is a seductive sort of smile, but it just makes her seem even more drunk.

Weirder and weirder.

'No need. We're cool.' I turn and grab my coat from the back of my chair, determined not to look at her again. Partially to save her from embarrassment, but mostly because I suspect my face will give away how freaked out I'm feeling right now.

'It's no big deal,' she says behind me.

I turn back to see her grasp at the hem of her t-shirt, which takes a couple of goes, then whip it up over her head. It gets stuck for a second around her chin, but she gives it an extra-hard yank and it comes free. She tosses it across the room towards Bea's desk, but misses her mark and it ends up on the floor by the bin.

I avert my gaze, sharpish. I daren't look at her. My blood is hot in my veins and I have a strange nervy flutter in my stomach. Probably because I have absolutely no idea what's going on here, or how to stop it.

'Dee, for God's sake, put your clothes back on,' I mutter,

concentrating on pushing my noncompliant arm through the armhole of my coat.

'Come on, Jem. Loosen up! I'm just trying to make friends with you.'

I sense her moving towards me and my heartrate accelerates. Is she doing this to deliberately make me uncomfortable? For the fun of it? I wouldn't put it past her.

Continuing to ignore her – the best thing all round at this juncture, I feel – I'm about to walk away from my desk and head at top speed for the door, when she lurches into my path, bringing me up short.

I have no choice but to look at her now.

'Wait. Don't go. Not yet.'

'I have to. It's knocking-off time,' I mutter through numb lips.

She's staring at my mouth now in riveted fascination.

'Have you kissed my sister?' she asks.

'No,' I say quickly.

'Not yet,' she corrects me, raising one suggestive eyebrow. 'But you want to. You've thought about it.' It's not a question.

'I'm not discussing this with you any more. I have to go.'

But as I move to the side, she mirrors the action and my momentum moves me closer to her, so we're only inches apart now.

Then she seems to stumble forwards and our mouths connect for a moment, her lips soft and warm against mine.

I'm so stunned, I don't react right away and we gaze into each other's eyes, our breathing accelerated. Seeming to take this as acceptance, she moves forwards and presses her mouth to mine again, sliding her hands up my neck and round to cup the back of my head. For one crazy moment, I let her kiss me, enjoying the feel of intimate human contact.

I breathe in the citrusy scent of her and my entire body rushes with electric heat. I feel myself get hard.

It's unexpected and utterly baffling.

And I know I have to stop this. She's clearly not in her right mind. I can't let it go any further.

Even if I wanted to.

Which I don't.

I jerk away from her and I feel her hands slide away from where they were gripping the back of my head.

She's staring at me now like she can't compute why I'm stopping her from kissing me.

'Dee! What the hell?' I say, my voice rasping through my throat. What is she doing to me? I've never felt so freaked.

'Oh. Um. Sorry,' she mutters. She looks unsure of herself now, like she's confused about what just happened.

I move away from her and go to scoop her t-shirt up from the floor, trying to ignore the way my lips are tingling. My skin feels alive with a prickling sensation I've never experienced before and I'm desperately hoping my erection goes down quickly before she notices it.

'Here. Put this back on,' I say, thrusting the t-shirt towards her, keeping my eyes firmly on her face.

'Okay,' she says, grabbing it from me.

I turn away and stare at the wall while – I hope – she pulls it back on over her head.

When I dare to look back at her, I'm relieved to see she's fully dressed again.

Her eyes still have that hazy look about them, which makes me pretty sure she's under the influence of something.

She might love to tease and taunt me for fun, but she's never gone this far before. There has to be more to it than bog-standard antagonism.

'Are you drunk?' I ask.

'No!' She actually seems offended by this suggestion. 'I've not drunk any alcohol for a week.' She takes a couple of stumbling steps back and sits on the edge of my desk, folding her arms and giving me an insouciant stare.

But there's definitely something not right here. I'm sure of it.

'Did you take something, then? Other than paracetamol, I mean.'

'I did, as a matter of fact. I took some of the painkillers my mum takes for her bad back sometimes. She gave them to me the other day when I pulled a muscle in my shoulder. Lucky for me that she did. They've completely stopped my ankle from hurting. I can't feel a thing now.'

'I'm guessing you've taken Tramadol?'

'Yup. That's the one.'

I let out a sigh and shake my head. 'You idiot! You shouldn't take drugs prescribed for someone else.'

She frowns. 'Okay, Mr Binary. No need to be a dick about it. I feel fine. I only took the dose it recommended on the packet.'

Well, at least that explains the irrational behaviour.

'Hmm, well, I don't think opiates are the drug for you. They seem to be making you even less inhibited than usual.'

She bats a hand at me, but it's a less precise movement than she'd normally execute and it looks like she's doing it in slow motion. 'Oh, Jem. What must it be like to live in your sensible, follow-the-instructions-to-the-letter world? Are you ever *naughty*?'

I tense at her teasing tone.

Oh man, where's she going with this?

'Seriously, Dee. You should leave the room before you do or say something else you regret later.'

She throws up her hands, again in slow motion. 'Okay. Fine. If you're not going to be friendly, I *will* leave.'

'Good.'

'I'll go back to my room and stare at the wall.'

'Probably for the best.'

We're glaring at each other again now. It feels as if we're trapped in a battle of wills. Who will look away first?

Well, it's not going to be me. I could do this for hours if I have to. I like to win.

A few more beats pass, before I see a small frown flitter across her brow.

Then she swallows hard.

Finally, her shoulders slump and her gaze drops.

As I watch this happen, it suddenly occurs to me that the previous high colour on her cheeks has drained away. She looks a bit pale. No. She looks a bit green.

'Are you okay?' I ask.

'Um.' She gives her head a little shake then seems to regret it. Lifting a hand to cover her mouth, she says, 'Feel a bit sick, actually,' behind it.

Ah.

I've heard opiate painkillers can make you feel nauseous.

'Just going to...' she mutters, before launching herself away from my desk and scurrying quickly out of the room.

I hear the door to the bathroom slam, then the muffled, unsettling sound of Dee vomiting.

Ugh.

What am I meant to do now? Should I go in there and hold her hair back?

No. That would be weird. I should wait for her to come out and check she's okay, though.

It's a few more minutes before she leaves the bathroom, looking a bit less pale now.

I'm waiting for her in the hall with a glass of water and she takes it gratefully from me and swallows a big gulp of it.

'Thanks.'

'Welcome,' I say gently. 'How are you feeling now?'

'Not great. Embarrassed. I think I should probably go and lie down.' She glances towards the bedroom door, then back at me. 'Uh. Honestly, I'm actually feeling a bit wobbly.'

To my horror, her eyes fill with tears.

Oh, man. I have no idea how to deal with a crying woman.

'Will you stay with me for a bit?' she asks in a small voice. 'I really don't want to be on my own when I'm feeling like this.'

I look down at the ground, trying to formulate a response. I know I can't just leave her alone now, not when she's feeling scared and ill. What kind of a person would do that? Not one I want to be.

'Please?' she says to the top of my head. 'I won't try to kiss you again, I promise.'

How am I supposed to respond to that? I don't want her to kiss me, obviously, but I don't want to be mean about it to her face.

I huff out a sigh. 'Okay. Fine. Just for a bit. I've still got a tonne of work I want to get through tonight when I get home. I've not done as much as I wanted today, what with all the interruptions.'

Her nod is sheepish, but then she gives me a warm, grateful smile.

There's an odd fluttering feeling in my chest at the sight of her being so vulnerable with me. This is not the Dee I usually get. But I can't let her manipulate me. I've seen how she does it to Bea and there's no way I'm letting her do it to me too.

'You know, you need to stop doing the first wild thing that

comes into your head before considering the consequences,' I state crossly. Though as soon as the words are out of my mouth, I regret saying them. I sound like a total dick.

The smile drops from her mouth.

'I made a mistake. One I won't be making again,' she says, before hobbling away from me, into the bedroom.

I follow her in there and watch as she gets into Bea's bed and pulls the duvet over herself, turning away from me.

I sit down on the other side. 'Okay. Well, good,' I say in a kinder tone this time, shuffling down the mattress so I can lie down next to her. A break from the screen would actually be welcome right now. I've been coding pretty solidly for the last few days and my eyes feel gritty and tired.

'Jem?' comes a small voice from within the duvet.

'Yeah?'

'Thanks for staying,' she says.

'Sure.'

'It's kind of you.'

'Hmm.'

There's an unusual tension in my chest now and another feeling I can't quite put my finger on. But whatever. Anyone would have done the same and stayed with her. Anyone with a shred of decency, anyway.

It's not long before I hear the gentle snuffling sounds of Dee's breathing as it slows right down and she falls asleep.

I'll just wait for a few more minutes to make sure she doesn't wake up and need to puke again.

It's a bit cool in the bedroom, so I pull the edge of the duvet over me and stare up at the ceiling, wondering how Bea's doing.

I hope things get back to normal soon is the last thing I think before I close my eyes for a second to rest them.

I don't open them again until I wake with a start to find Bea and Dee's father standing next to the bed in the faint morning light, with one eyebrow arched and an expression of reproach on his face.

5

DELILAH

I wake up with a start.

Someone's saying my name in an urgent tone that sends a rush of anxiety straight through me.

'What? What's wrong?' I say, fighting through my grogginess to wake up fully and deal with whatever emergency I'm being dragged into.

'Your dad's here,' the voice says.

I know that voice, but I can't quite place it. And where the hell am I? This doesn't feel like my bedroom. It doesn't smell like it either. I don't use this brand of laundry detergent. It smells more like Bea.

Ah, yes. I'm in Bea's bed. Staying in her flat. I'm reminded why when I shift my legs and my still-swollen ankle gives a throb of pain.

Ugh.

Why do I feel so rough?

Then it all comes flooding back and my body heats like I've stepped into a furnace.

Oh no.

What the hell did I do?

I took some of those painkillers Mum gave me, that's what, and I think they were a bit strong.

I felt great at first, really happy and positive. Confident enough to get on with my marketing plan even, which in those moments, I suspected probably wasn't as bad as Jonah was making out. I felt sure I could fix it, anyway.

So, I went into the office.

I'd wanted to show Jem I'm just as cool and as serious a person as my sister.

Who he's probably in love with.

Huh.

I'm not sure why I find that so upsetting.

But discovering that photo he'd taken of her on his phone had fried my brain.

Of course, it shouldn't be a surprise he's in love with Bea. Most men find her incredibly attractive, but I hadn't counted on Jem feeling that way about her too.

But when I saw him standing there by his desk in the shadows, all broad shoulders and frowny, dark-eyed glare, ready to walk out on me, something weird happened. I suddenly forgot what I went in there for and all I could think about was him and my sister together and how protective that made me feel.

And then...

And then...

I tried to seduce Jem.

Jem.

Of all people.

To warn him off, maybe.

Hmm. I'm not exactly sure why I did it. I wanted to shake him up, I think. And get him to stop thinking about my sister as a viable partner.

And I guess the shaking-up bit worked. From what I remember, he certainly seemed pretty freaked out by my rather rash ploy.

But that doesn't explain why he's in bed with me.

I roll over to find him sitting up on the other side of the mattress, his dark, wavy hair a mess and the look in his eyes a bit wild.

Lordy lord. How strange it is that Jem having stubble on his jaw makes him suddenly seem sexy.

Wait. Stop. No more thoughts like that, thanks.

Because he's definitely not thinking about how sexy I look in the mornings.

In fact, it appears, from the confusion on his face, that he's not sure what he's doing here either.

'What did you say?' I ask him, aware in the back of my brain that there's still some emergency I need to deal with – other than finding Jem in bed with me, that is.

'Your dad just came into the room, looking for Bea. I explained it was you in here with me and he walked out, saying he'd put the kettle on and wait for us to get up. I get the feeling he's not exactly pleased to find the two of us in bed together. We're going to have to explain he's made a mistake. I don't want him thinking I'm taking advantage of... err, *things* when I'm in business with your sister. I definitely don't need him as an enemy. So we need to get out there and explain – this.' He waves his hand between us, an expression of dismay on his face.

Ugh. That's all I need. My dad turning up right now and needing an *explanation*.

My *bloody* dad.

Bane of my life.

He's always sticking his nose into my business and I'm sick of it. Anyway, so what if I'm in bed with Jem? It's none of his concern.

But I guess that's not how Jem sees it.

'Why *are* you here?' I ask him, my voice still rough with sleep. I'm a bit hazy about what happened after I was sick last night. I remember getting into bed, but I'm not sure why Jem's here with me.

'I didn't want to leave you alone when you were ill. You asked me to stay, remember? I just lay down next to you for a few minutes and I must have fallen asleep.'

'Oh. Right.' I think I remember that now. I was pretty discombobulated last night.

We stare at each other for a second.

This is so bizarre.

'And my dad thinks, what? That we're a couple?'

His shrug looks stiff and awkward. 'I guess so. Until we disabuse him of the notion.'

'Well, tough. I'm not inclined to explain my love life to my dad,' I say archly.

'But this isn't your love life,' Jem points out. 'I'm not your... you know... your...'

'Lover,' I finish for him. Apparently, it's too icky an idea for him to voice.

'Exactly.'

I suck in a breath. 'So how are we going to explain this then?' I ask.

He raises his first eyebrow of the day at me.

'No,' I say. 'There's no way I'm telling him how this really happened. I've only just managed to convince him I'm not a total loser and if he finds out I took some of Mum's meds, he's going to do his nut. I already have to think up a plausible excuse for why it's me here, in Bea's flat – not doing my job – and why Bea's MIA.'

'So, what? You're going to lie to your dad?' he asks.

'Got it in one,' I confirm.

'And how do you expect to get away with that? Surely he's not going to believe it?' Jem says, clearly not anticipating an affirmative answer to that.

'He is if you back me up,' I point out. The only way to handle this is to style it out, I've decided. Maybe if I go at it with enough energy, I'll somehow manifest a positive outcome.

Okay, I know I'm reaching right now, but I've just woken up, I'm in pain and I've got nothing else to lose.

'So, you're asking me to pretend that we're actually in a relationship – and what? That it's serious?' Jem says, his expression incredulous.

'Well, yes, and that you're staying here with me because of my injury,' I say, scrabbling for an argument. 'If he finds out Bea's off pretending to be me and doing my job, it's not going to reflect well on any of us, is it?' I say, giving him a beseeching look. 'You included. Because you're just as involved in this as we are now. So, perhaps we could just make it *seem* like we're together at the moment and *suggest* that Bea's off doing something important, like – I don't know – attending a good friend's mum's funeral in Scotland or something. Something he won't want to question for fear of seeming like a dick.'

I stare at him, wondering what kind of reaction I'm going to get to this verbal incontinence and I'm surprised to see he doesn't shake his head in refusal at me.

Instead, he seems to be considering what I've said.

I guess he's concerned about this looking bad for Bea as well as himself.

'Hmm.'

'Hmm?' I say, raising my eyebrows in a hopeful manner. 'Look, it's just going to be a bit of make-believe, for a really short amount of time. No biggie. You don't have to drape yourself all over me or anything. Affection can be kept to an absolute minimum. We'll act like we're one of those cool and grown-up kind of couples.'

He huffs out a breath. 'Yeah. Okay. I guess we could just go with that for now. But we'll let him know we've "broken up" the moment a decent amount of time has passed.' He puts his head in his hands and rubs his face against both palms. 'Ugh. What the hell,' he mutters to himself, then gives a short, sharp laugh.

I'm worried for a second that he's flipping out over this, but that concern is allayed when he turns to give me a tight smile, then blows out a long, low breath.

'Okay. Let's get this over with so we can get on with our day.'

There's a tight feeling in my chest now and I realise I'm on the edge of tears. What's that all about? I force the feeling down and nod back at him.

'Thanks, Jem. I owe you one.'

'You owe me more than one,' he says, getting up off the bed and tucking his crumpled shirt into his trousers.

I tear my gaze away as he tries to neaten up his hair too before facing my father.

What is it about seeing Jem undone like this that's making me feel so flustered?

Luckily, I don't need to dwell on that thought because after taking one last, steadying breath, he leaves the room and a moment later, I hear him greeting my dad in the kitchen with a friendly salutation.

I know I can't let Jem face the music on his own, so I struggle up out of bed and hobble after him, finding him and my dad facing each other across the kitchen table, three mugs of tea sitting in a row in front of them.

'So how long's this being going on for?' my dad asks, looking between the two of us, his expression implacable.

Why does he always have to be so grumpy about everything? Particularly everything I do.

'Not long,' I say, wanting to keep things vague so we don't trip ourselves up. 'Jem stayed with me last night because I've sprained my ankle and I'm incapacitated and in a lot of pain with it. Bea said I could crash here while she's away at a friend's mum's funeral in Scotland.'

My father's brow creases. 'She didn't tell me about that.'

'No, well, you're not her keeper any more, are you,' I point out, riled by his accusatory tone. 'And she only found out about it at the last minute,' I add when his scowl deepens at my insolence.

My father then does a very deliberate check of his watch. 'And aren't you meant to be hard at work at your new job at the hotel right now? Don't tell me you've been fired already?'

My body gives a shiver of hurt as I realise he's probably just been biding his time, waiting for me to announce I've lost the job he was apparently so proud of me securing. He obviously never expected me to keep it for long.

This makes me even more determined to prove him wrong.

'I'm working from home because the hotel's closed for a few days while we have the bed bugs bombed,' I say wildly.

My father's eyes widen. 'Really?' He looks horrified by this. 'That doesn't sound good.'

'It's fine,' I say, batting a hand. 'Mostly precautionary, to be honest. It's off season so we're very quiet.'

'Hmm,' is all he says in response.

Does he suspect that's bullshit? Probably. But I don't care. I just want him gone.

'Anyway, why are you here? And what makes you think it's okay to just storm into Bea's bedroom?'

'I didn't storm in. I knocked, then waited, knocked again, then came in, thinking the room was empty, only to find you and' – he turns to glare at Jem now – '*him* in there. I thought for a second it was Bea in bed with you' – he directs this fully at Jem now – 'which, as a business decision, would have been spectacularly bad, in my opinion,' he says, like his opinion is all that matters.

Jem shrugs, though his shoulders look tense so it seems a bit awkward. 'I agree. Which is why I'm not sleeping with Bea.'

'But you are sleeping with my other daughter,' my dad says, leaning back in his chair and folding his arms, like he's acting the big boss in his own office, rather than being a gooseberry in Bea's kitchen. 'I'm not sure that's such a great move at this juncture of your career either. What if you split up and it causes a rift with Bea? What happens to the start-up then?' His tone holds an undertone of incredulity now, which only serves to make me madder.

Is he suggesting Jem's making a mistake getting involved with me? Charming. Even if it is only make-believe at the moment, I'm still hurt by his reaction.

Jem must dislike his rancour too because he folds his arms in a mirror image of my dad and says, 'We're all adults. We can make our own decisions on that score.'

Seeing him standing up to my dad gives me a thrill of pleasure and I'm aware of my blood pulsing harder through my veins and an unexpected, stirring pressure between my thighs. I didn't know Jem had it in him. But maybe he's only reacting to the insinuation that he'd be putting Bea in a difficult position and I barely figure in this equation.

My father just lets out a long-suffering sigh. 'Okay, fine. I didn't come here to discuss your love life. I'm here to see Bea. I need her to come away with me for a couple of days on a business trip.'

Both Jem and I stare at my dad in confusion.

Jem pulls himself together first. 'Well, Bea's not here at the moment. As Dee said, she's away for a few days, so she's not free to do that.'

My father just rubs his hand over his face like this is the worst news he's had in a long time. 'Dammit,' he mutters into his palm.

'Why do you need Bea to go?' I ask, intrigued to see my dad looking so discouraged. He's very rarely out of control, in any part of his life. Which is why he and my mum were always doomed to fail as a couple. She's way too flaky for him. I guess it was her beauty and charisma that snagged his attention when they first got together, and when she fell pregnant with Bea and me after they'd only been dating for a few weeks, my dad did the 'honourable thing' and asked her to marry him.

The rest is some very difficult history.

'There's a guy that I've been trying to persuade to take on a non-exec directorship for a while,' my dad says, dropping his hands back into his lap and seeming to regain his poise. 'He's a business titan and extremely well connected and would be a real asset to have on board. I've finally managed to pin him down for a meeting but he wants me to go to him, where he's staying on his private Greek Island, for discussions because he's time-poor at the moment. He's off to climb Kilimanjaro soon and this is the only window he has.' He pushes his fingers through his hair in agitation. 'He's well-known for having strong family values, so I thought I'd take Bea along to help me with the charm offensive. He seemed keen to meet her when I suggested it. I guess he probably thinks it'll give him an insight into me as a man.'

Huh. *Her.* Not her *and* me. Just Bea. I guess he doesn't consider me charming enough.

My dad suddenly realises what he's just implied by this too, because he glances at me and says, 'I thought you'd be caught up at the hotel, so not available.' At least he tries to sound convincing.

I'm not fooled, though. It wouldn't have occurred to him for a second to ask me to go with him to help out.

This makes me inexplicably angry. And sad. And resolute. I'm going to prove the guy wrong someday, even if it kills me.

'Perhaps I should just give Bea a call and find out when she'll be done there,' my dad says, starting to pull his mobile out of his pocket.

'No!' I shout, making him jump. 'I mean, you shouldn't. She's set on being there for her friend whose mum just *died*. You can't go bothering her now. Knowing Bea, she'll feel terrible about not being able to help you and it'll totally stress her out. You don't want to do that to her, right?'

His hand is still on his mobile, as if he's not sure whether to ignore my protests.

Drastic measures are in order.

'But, luckily for you, I'm as free as a bird for a couple of days, Dad, so I'd be happy to come with you to a private Greek island and charm a boomer,' I say with a forced smile.

I think I can actually see all my father's many conflicting thoughts skitter across his face as he tries to think up some excuse as to why he doesn't want my help.

But I know why. He doesn't trust me not to mess this up for him. He thinks I'll bad-mouth him in front of his business buddy and make him look like a fool – and the poor father figure he is.

There's the sound of a low cough beside me and I'm suddenly intensely aware that Jem's watching this whole charade. I flush with embarrassment. He's seeing first-hand how little my dad thinks of me and my skills and charm now – not just in a business sense, but as a member of his own family.

Great. That's all I need.

'I'd be happy to come along and support you too,' I hear Jem say in what sounds like a completely serious tone.

Both my father and I turn to stare at him in surprise.

'I can work remotely while we're there,' Jem continues. 'And I'd be very interested to see how these types of business connections are made. Learn from the best. It's not something I've had much experience with yet and I'd like to improve my networking skills. I'm sure it'll benefit my and Bea's venture in the future.'

Turning back to look at my dad, I can see from the way his eyes have lit up that he's into the idea of this. Jem will save the day.

Bloody Jem.

Boy wonder.

I know I'm being churlish and that I should be very grateful to him right now, but the sting of humiliation is still prickling my skin, so I'm not able to get there just yet.

'Yes, okay. That could work. You could go as Bea's proxy,' my dad says. 'I've already told Jeff about the start-up you're growing with her so he'll be interested to meet you. And being Dee's, err, partner will probably be a help too, in terms of us looking like a strong family unit.'

He gives another nod, as if he's settled in his mind about the benefits of that decision. He's always liked and got on with Jem, so they'll be able to talk business the whole time.

Oh joy.

'Look, Dee, I appreciate you saying you'll do this for me,' Dad says, turning to me now. 'And if you treat this completely seriously and help me pull it off, I'll pay off your student loan. Fair deal?'

I'm stunned. He must really need this to work if he's giving me an incentive like that not to show him up.

'Okay. It's a deal,' I say. Not that I exactly have a choice. It might look odd to refuse it and I want him less suspicious of my offer to help, not more.

Dad nods. 'That's decided then. I'll pick you both up at eleven. Jeff's sending his private plane to fly us over to mainland Greece, then we'll chopper over to the island.'

My head starts to spin. What the hell have we just walked into? An episode of *Succession*?

Luckily, Jem has his wits about him because he nods and says, 'Okay, great. We'll be ready.'

'You both have passports?' my dad asks, getting up from the kitchen table.

'Yes.'

'Yup.'

'Good. See you later.'

And with that, my dad strides out of the room, then vacates the building, shutting the door loudly behind him.

I turn to look at Jem. 'Did that really just happen?' I ask in a rush of breath.

'Yeah,' Jem says, sounding a bit less confident now that my dad has gone.

'Are you really okay to go along with this?'

There's a pause where I wonder whether he's changed his mind and is about to run after my dad and make some excuse as to why, actually, he can't go through with this crazy plan.

But he doesn't.

'Yes,' he says again. 'It's only for a couple of days, right? And I meant what I said about it being a good opportunity to network. But I need to make a call and go home to pack a few things first. Do you need anything picking up from your flat?'

I blink at him. He's efficiency personified. No wonder he gets on so well with my sister. 'How can you be so practical about all this?' I ask, shaking my head in wonder.

'Needs must.' He pauses again. 'And practice.'

I just nod, then go to grab a pen and piece of paper to write down all the things I need him to pick up from my flat – including my passport – and where to find them. I cringe a little inside as I realise he's going to need to rummage in my underwear drawer to pack me some pants and bras.

Oh well, he's the one that suggested this.

I hand him the piece of paper, then limp off and return with a set of keys to my flat. 'There you go. I've written my address down too.'

'Great.'

'And I'll call Bea and let her know what's going on.'

'Good idea. We don't want her phoning your dad for something and giving the game away.' He rubs his hand over his brow. 'God knows what she's going to make of all this.'

Turning away from me, he heads for the door.

'I was interested to hear you say that getting together with Bea would be bad for business,' I blurt at his back.

He turns to raise that inevitable eyebrow at me. 'I'm not discussing that subject any more, so give it a rest, okay.'

I just flash him a smile, though my insides are squirming.

He gives me a hard stare, then starts walking away again.

'Jem,' I call after him.

Sighing, he spins around and looks at me, impatience written across his face – and something else. Something I can't quite make out. 'Yeah?'

'Look, I'm sorry about my appalling behaviour last night. I can't believe I acted like that. It wasn't okay,' I say, grimacing. 'I don't know what got into me.' I screw up my nose. 'Well, actually, I do of course: meds not meant for me. They really messed with my head.'

Before he can respond, I hold up a hand. 'Not that that's a

good excuse. You were right, I shouldn't have taken them. It was a stupid thing to do.'

After a moment's tense silence, he just nods, his mouth set into a firm line. 'It's okay. Let's just forget it happened.' He takes a breath, then adds, 'I appreciate the apology.'

I nod back and swallow hard, grateful for his compassion. 'And thanks for doing this. I owe you *many more* than one.'

'Yes, you do,' is all he says back, before leaving me alone in the kitchen wondering how the *heck* I always manage to get myself into such crazy situations.

6

JEM

When I woke up this morning, I never imagined my life would have taken such a wild turn. But then, I woke up next to Dee, so it always had the potential to veer towards the absurd.

I take a break from working to glance out of the window of the luxury private plane Tim Donovan has invited us to join him on, in order to execute a charm offensive on what turns out to be one of the most influential titans of business to walk the planet: Sir Jeff Blackmore.

The plush leather armchairs and soft wool carpets in the cabin look – and smell – new.

In fact, it reeks of money in here. It's all understated interior design and sophistication.

Aspirational as fuck.

Not that it's ever been one of my life goals to own a private jet. I just want enough money to be secure. I want to know I can get myself – and anyone I love – out of trouble if I need to. I'm not interested in owning a fleet of sports cars or a mansion in every country; I just want to feel safe.

Speaking of feeling safe, I'm not entirely sure what made me say I'd come along on this trip. I think it was something to do with the look on Dee's face when her dad had been about to dismiss her offer of help. I felt a pang, deep in my chest, seeing her dismayed reaction. Bea's always told me that their dad plays favourites, but I've never actually seen it before.

And it felt pretty brutal.

But maybe Dee was just worried she was going to be found out and her reaction was more about being desperate to keep up the ruse she and Bea have going.

I don't know. I can't work her out.

But I didn't want Bea to have to deal with this, so I stepped in on her behalf. As a friend.

I get why Tim might have paused when Dee suggested that she go in Bea's place, though. They've always had a combative relationship, which isn't the look Tim's going for in front of such an influential business connection. I guess he'll be hoping that I act as a buffer between him and Dee and – what? – keep her in line?

Ha. No chance. Not Dee.

There's no way she'd listen to me.

Not that I'd ever attempt to control anything she does. I wouldn't do that to anyone, let alone someone as wilful as Delilah.

Closing the lid of my laptop, which I've been coding on since we took off, and looking over at her, I see she's staring down at her mobile, reading an e-book on the screen. Her nose is wrinkled in concentration and a weird zing of pleasure hits me out of nowhere.

But it won't be because she looks cute when she's clearly getting a kick out of what she's reading.

It's more likely to be the fact I'm here on a private plane on the way to a Greek island, soon to be in the company of a major player in the world of business, that's got me excited.

Yeah, that'll be it.

As far as I'm aware, Tim hasn't looked up from his mobile screen for the entirety of the journey so far either. He gave us the run-down of what he expects from us while we were waiting in the private lounge for the plane to be ready to board and hasn't talked to us since.

I suspect he's now doing a deep dive into anything he can find online that'll help him win Blackmore over. He's not got to the position he has without putting in the hours, after all.

I can see why Bea's so inspired by him.

He's a powerhouse of a man.

* * *

The rest of the flight is smooth and we land exactly at the time we were told we would. The whole thing's a professional operation from start to finish – but then, if you're worth billions like Sir Jeff, you probably command so much respect, no one wants to disappoint or inconvenience you.

I can only dream about having that sort of status.

After disembarking, we're driven by limo to another part of the private airport where a sleek, black helicopter is waiting to take us to Kapheira Island. According to Tim, the island's been in the possession of Blackmore since the mid-eighties. He used to lend it out to wealthy, elite families and royalty so they could holiday unbothered by paparazzi, but he's stopped doing that now and only entertains friends and business acquaintances there.

So we're honoured to be invited.

Dee's been unusually quiet for the whole journey, which is

making me a little nervous. I know she's still in pain with her ankle – and has been grudgingly letting me help her get up and down any steps she can't manage whilst using her crutches – but even so, it's not like her to be this morose.

I wonder whether it's something to do with being in her father's company? Being around him seems to have turned her into a sullen teenager.

You see, that's what I love about Bea: she doesn't need looking after. I could never see myself with someone as high maintenance as Dee. I have enough on my plate looking after Mum as it is.

I glance over at Dee as the helicopter lifts away from the ground and she gives me a tight smile, her eyes a little wider than usual.

Is she nervous?

'You okay?' I mouth.

She nods, then leans towards me so she can speak directly into my ear, bringing her distinctive citrusy scent with her.

'Honestly, I'm not the biggest fan of air travel. But don't let on to my dad, okay.' She pulls back to give me a stern warning look.

I return her nod. Huh, well that's a surprise. I didn't think Delilah Donovan was afraid of anything.

Looking down at her hands clasped in her lap, I realise she's gripping them together so hard, they're turning white.

Instinctively, I reach over and put one of my own onto hers.

She shoots me a look, her brows pinched, then to my surprise, unlocks her hands and slides one into mine, squeezing it tightly.

'Thanks,' she mutters, her smile stiff, but genuine.

For the rest of the twenty-minute journey, her hand remains in mine. It's the strangest thing, holding hands with Dee. Another thing I thought I'd never do. It's both comforting and weirdly compelling.

I tell myself not to think about how her mouth felt pressed firmly to mine last night when she came on to me in the office. But my mind won't comply. And neither will my body.

I shift a little in the seat to disguise the physical reaction I'm experiencing at the memory of it.

This is not the time or place for that, I tell myself sternly. *Get a bloody grip!*

As the island comes into view, I lean towards the window to gaze out at it to distract myself. I'd estimate it's only about twenty acres in size, with a large house and a scattering of outbuildings sitting right in the centre, on top of a hill. The majority of the rest of it is covered in trees, apart from a large area of lawn and land-scaped gardens ringing the house, and there's a clearly defined road leading down to a long sand beach in the north.

Dee's grip tightens as we swiftly descend onto a helipad on the lawn.

The moment we're down, she removes her rather sweaty hand from mine and starts fiddling about with the buckle of her seatbelt.

There's an almost manic sort of energy to her now and I lay my hand onto her arm to attempt to reassure her this is going to be okay.

She shrugs me off. Not in an obvious way, so her dad will see, but in a subtle twitch and tension in her arm, like she doesn't want me patronising her. Apparently, it was fine me comforting her while we were in the air, but now we're on solid ground, she's regained her bravado.

I don't know why it bothers me so much, but it does. I was only trying to be friendly.

But then, we're not friends. We don't seem to be able to be.

'Okay then. Let's get this done,' Tim says on the other side of me, like he's about to go to war.

When both Dee and I look round at him, he fixes us with a stern look, his gaze darting between us. 'Let me do most of the talking, and take my lead. Remember, we need to project a strong family unit here.'

'All right, Dad, I know what needs to be done,' Dee replies with an undertone of irritation. 'I promise to be on my best behaviour.'

Tim just raises his eyebrows at her, which manages to convey exactly how unsure he is of both of those statements.

'Don't worry, we're all on the same page, Tim,' I say to draw fire away from the conflict brewing between them.

Hmm. Perhaps I've bitten off more than I can chew here, being around these two.

Still, there's nothing I can do about it now.

There's a tense pause before Tim says, 'Okay then. Well, let's get this show on the road.' Then he opens the door of the helicopter and hops out, immediately striding away towards a couple of men who are waiting at the edge of the lawn to greet us.

Dee rolls her eyes at me and I shoot her a tight smile before we too step out of the helicopter and follow her father into the fray.

* * *

Sir Jeff Blackmore turns out to be a good guy.

He's certainly very welcoming and surprisingly down to earth as he greets us all with a warm smile and a firm shake of the hand, saying, 'Call me Jeff,' before leading us through the mani-cured garden. He stops to point out some of his favourite plants and shrubs, before ushering us into the mansion he calls home on this rugged but beautiful island.

The house has been built in the Cycladic style, like the places covering the island of Mykonos that I've seen multiple reels of on my social media channels recently. It's made up of cubic shapes with whitewashed walls and large wooden doors and window frames. I guess it needs to stand strong against the fierce winds they get in this part of Europe, and this design lends itself well to that purpose.

Even though it's still late winter, the sun is out here and it's a temperate fifteen degrees centigrade. Warmer than in England anyway, that's for sure.

There are some dark clouds looming in the distance, so I wonder whether there's some rain on the way. Hopefully, it'll pass us by and let us enjoy some sunshine while we're here.

'We've put you all in the guest quarters in the west wing of the house,' Jeff says as we walk through a wide, tiled entrance hall. The walls are hung with expensive-looking modern art and the large, claw-footed table supporting an extravagant floral display is a highly polished antique, by the looks of it.

'You're welcome to use any of the facilities here, so don't feel forced to stay in your rooms.' He points to a door on the other side of the entrance hall. 'There's a pool and a gym through there.' Turning in the other direction, he waves towards another door. 'And the dining room and kitchens are through there. Just ask a member of staff if you ever want anything to eat or drink.' He spins back to face us with a smile. 'I'll let you freshen up and we'll reconvene for coffee in half an hour. How does that sound?'

'That sounds great, Jeff, thanks,' Tim says, following him as he heads off down a long corridor, away from the living area, which we catch a glimpse of as we pass by the open door to it. I clock a horseshoe configuration of leather sofas facing a huge TV screen in there before we hurry on after the two men to our rooms.

I'm itching to go and explore the place, but maybe there'll be time for that later.

'You're in here, Tim,' Jeff says to Dee's dad, opening a door to a grand-looking suite with views of the aquamarine Aegean Sea.

'And you two' – he leaves Tim standing at the door to his room and strides down the corridor, motioning for Dee and me to follow him – 'are in the room at the end.' He leans in towards Dee. 'To give you a bit of space away from your dad.' His eyes twinkle with mischief and I decide my initial take of him was correct. He's a decent guy.

He must be in his seventies, with a shock of silver hair and weathered skin, but he's the picture of health – and wealth. The casual suit he's wearing is understated and comfortable looking, but the cut shouts personal tailoring.

'I'm sure you'll be comfortable in here.'

Dee and I just nod and murmur in agreement, as we've been instructed to do.

Jeff ushers us into the room and explains that our bags have already been taken out of the helicopter and put in here by the guy in chinos that was standing with him when we arrived, who is apparently called Nico.

His butler of sorts.

Oh man, it's another world here.

It's only when Jeff's given us a final wave and shut the door behind him, and we're gazing at our own stunning view across the small island to the sparkling sea beyond, that it hits me that Dee and I are staying in the same room.

With only one king-sized bed.

We both turn to stare at it for a moment.

There's a strange pulsing silence in the room where neither of us seem to want to acknowledge the dilemma we find ourselves in.

But there's no need to panic. The room is huge and has a large, comfortable-looking sofa pushed up against the wall opposite. I can sleep on that for one night.

'I'll take the sofa,' Dee says before I can.

'Don't be ridiculous,' I scoff. 'You can't sleep on that with an injured ankle. I'll take it.'

She frowns at me for a second, then seems to accept the wisdom of my words. 'Okay. I guess that makes sense.'

Is she hiding a smile of relief? I wouldn't put it past her to only pretend she'd be happy to take it, but expect me to insist that I did.

Whatever. We can't both sleep in that bed; it would be too weird.

'So, this is a bit bloody awkward!' Dee says with a strained-sounding laugh.

I glance at her and see there's unease in her expression.

'You don't need to worry; I'm not a snorer, so I won't disturb you. And I'll stay strictly to my side of the room,' I joke, in an attempt to relieve the strange tension in the air. I'm not sure why we're both suddenly acting so bizarrely. Probably because we're tired from the journey and neither of us had considered the fact we'd be expected to share a bed. I'm not sure why not. I guess we'd not wanted to entertain the idea – until we were forced to.

'I know you will, Jem. You've made it perfectly clear you find the idea of sleeping with me abhorrent,' she says, also apparently going for a jokey tone, but it falls flat.

I swallow. My mouth is dry.

Spotting a bottle of mineral water on the table next to the bed, I walk to it and crack the seal, then pour it into two glasses. I hand one to Dee, then down my own, grateful for the reprieve of not having to talk to her for a few moments.

How the hell are we going to get through the next day or two?

It's going to be uncomfortable, especially as we'll be expected to pretend that we're a happy, newly minted couple.

I think back to the way she shrugged my hand off in the helicopter.

Hmm.

'Look,' I say, forcing calm confidence into my voice, 'we're going to need to show a united front for the next few hours, at least, so let's try and relax around each other, okay? It's going to look pretty bloody weird if we don't say a single word to each other and jump whenever we touch.'

She nods slowly. 'Yeah, you're right. We need to at least *seem* attracted to each other.'

'Yeah.'

'So, what are you saying?'

'I'm not saying anything, except try to relax around me.'

'So you're not asking for a practice snog then?' The corner of her mouth twitches up.

I let out a startled laugh. 'Err, no. That's not what I was suggesting.'

'Because we could, if you like. Have a quick go?'

'A *go*?' My mouth is dry again.

'Yeah. With both of us into the idea, this time. So we know how the other one kisses. Which way we turn our heads, for example, when we go in for a smacker. Just in case we need to do it in front of anyone later. It doesn't need to be a full-on snog. I was joking about that. Just a quick peck.'

She waggles both eyebrows at me and I feel laughter building in my chest. Or maybe it's hysteria.

No, no, no. This is not what I signed up for.

My skin's doing that weird prickling thing again.

Putting her glass down on the nearest flat surface, she turns to face me, her lips pressed together and her expression determined, then takes a deliberate step towards me.

My heart begins to hammer in my chest and I put up a halting hand. 'Whoa, there. That's really not necessary.'

'Just to be clear, I'd only be kissing you so I can prove to my dad I can be an asset to my family,' she says with a teasing grin.

'Sexy,' I say, suppressing my own smile. My heart gives a judder as she steps closer again and lifts her hands as if she's going to cup my face.

Before she can touch me, I take a decisive step backwards.

I can't let this happen. I won't be drawn into playing any more of her games. It would only complicate things.

I think she's doing this to teach me a lesson – that she'll get what she wants eventually, even if she has to be inventive about it.

I have to admit a grudging respect for her determination.

But if I do ever get the chance to be with Bea, I don't want having had any kind of *history* with Dee to get in the way.

So that's why I move deliberately away from her, even though it's a lot tougher to do than I thought it would be.

In fact, I'm hard again. Which I guess is just a human reaction to the idea of kissing, but it still troubles me that my body is responding this way. I really don't want her to know the effect her suggestion has had on me, so I turn away and grab my bag, then head straight for a door on the other side of the room, which I'm hoping is our bathroom.

'Are you running away from me? It can't be that horrifying an idea to kiss me,' Dee jokes, but I hear a ring of hurt in her voice.

Turning my head – but not my body – I say, 'Course not. But we should get ready for that meeting with your dad and Jeff,' in a somewhat strangled voice.

I don't wait for her response and stride into the bathroom, shutting the door firmly behind me.

7

DELILAH

It could give a girl a complex, that kind of behaviour.

But I'm sure Jem was just making another of his points. That he's not prepared to do anything more than he's comfortable with.

I have to admit, I was just larking around at first, but perhaps I pushed the suggestion of the kiss further than I should have. I guess I was still smarting a little from him rejecting me when I tried to kiss him last night and I think I was trying to even us up, or perhaps get some sort of revenge on him for it.

Juvenile, I know.

So it's fine that he shut it down. Again.

As soon as he comes out of the bathroom, showered and looking like his usual put-together self, I go in there to freshen up from the journey and redo my make-up and by the time I've neatened myself up and my pulse has calmed down, my dad is knocking on our door, demanding we go with him to meet Jeff for that coffee and a chat.

The man himself is waiting for us in the sitting room, reading something on his phone, and he gestures for us to join him on the sofas. We all go to sit in a row opposite him, which feels a bit weird, so I get up and sit in an armchair to his left instead, making my dad and Jem the main focus of his attention. I'm intending to just sit back and stare out of the window while they talk business, as my dad made it plain he wants me to keep my mouth shut and just simper and smile at his side like an adoring daughter while he takes care of the chat.

But hey, if it means I get my student loan paid off, that's absolutely fine by me.

I glance at Jem and my lips give a tingle as I remember how close I was to kissing him only a few minutes ago. I really should rein in the teasing, but it's like a compulsion with me and him now. And it's actually kinda fun to see him squirm.

Attempting to clear my head, I sit back in my chair and place my hands in my lap, trying to look engaged, but demure. Exactly how my father wishes I'd always act.

My dad, in his inimitable way, launches straight into why he's here, trying to persuade Jeff his business is the next big thing and that they'd both benefit greatly if Jeff were to agree to take a seat on the executive board.

Jeff nods along for a while, before turning to fix Jem with a discerning stare.

'Jeremy, was it?'

'Just Jem. I've never used my full name. My dad was Jeremy.'

'Was?'

Jem shifts in his seat. 'Yeah. He died of a heart attack three years ago.'

My heart does a slow flip. I didn't know this. But then Jem and I have never really talked about anything important. And Bea's never told me any personal stuff about him. She's circumspect about her friends' private lives and totally not into gossip.

'I'm sorry to hear that,' Jeff says.

'Thank you.'

I steal a glance at my dad. He's looking a little thunderstruck too at the attention being diverted so blatantly away from him and his mission.

Ha. Well, maybe he'll learn that not everything has to be about business all the time.

'So that must have happened while you were at university?' Jeff asks, not seeming at all bothered by this swerve in conversation. In fact, he seems much more interested in finding out all about Jem rather than the business proposition my dad has for him. But then Dad did warn us that Jeff is into family dynamics and that's what we're here for after all – to help charm the pants off him – or rather his pants into a seat at my dad's table.

'That's right,' Jem says. 'During my first year.'

'Tough time to lose a parent. Not that there's ever a good time, of course. You have my sympathy,' Jeff says with a respectful nod in Jem's direction.

Jem nods back, then shrugs, his expression rueful. 'He'd had a good life and he'd been really ill for a while. My parents had me when they were quite old, after trying to get pregnant for years.'

'And how has your mother coped with losing him?' Jeff asks gently.

Jem pauses for a few beats and I see colour rise to his face. He opens his mouth, glances towards me, then looks back at Jeff again.

'Err. She's had early onset Alzheimer's for a while now, so she often forgets that he died.'

'Oh, I'm so sorry. Horrific disease.' It's Jeff's turn to pause now, before saying, 'Do you have any siblings to share the load?' His question is gentle, but direct. He's clearly not a man to mince his words.

'No. It's just me.'

'Forgive me for all the prying,' Jeff says, 'but does that mean you were the sole carer for them before going to university?'

'Yeah, I was,' Jem says. 'We didn't have the money to hire any help outside of the nursing that the NHS provided so I did a lot of the chores and care at home and looked after the finances. I guess it taught me how to look after myself from an early age though, so that's been a benefit. Especially as I'm running my own business now, with Bea.'

I'm aware I'm staring at Jem with my mouth open and when he glances at me again, I snap it shut and sit up straighter. There's a burning pressure in my throat and I give a low cough to try and get rid of it.

But it won't budge.

'I had a pretty tough childhood myself,' Jeff says. 'It set me in good stead for making something of myself as well. I'm glad to hear you're on a similar path. You're an impressive young man and I suspect you'll be very successful in whatever you do with an attitude like that,' he says, fixing Jem with his warm, twinkly gaze.

Jem, for once, seems lost for words and there's an awkward silence where he shifts in his seat, seemingly unable to respond to such forthright praise.

I feel a sudden urge to save him from his discomfort, but I'm not sure what to say. Perhaps a joke? But none come to mind.

I actually want to go over there and put my arms around him.

Luckily – and rather predictably – it's my father that rescues the conversation by first obsequiously agreeing with Jeff's praise, then bringing it back round to how they can best work together.

I tune out the business talk and let my mind swim with thoughts about what I just heard about Jem. Well, no wonder he's as uptight and controlled as he is. That's a hell of a way to grow up, and it must be awful to see his mum suffering with such a devastating disease.

I sneak a glance at him, but he's focused entirely on the conversation that Jeff and my dad are having and doesn't glance my way again once.

I watch him as he talks, finding a strange kind of pleasure in the fact I'm allowed to stare at him for as long as I like right now without it seeming weird.

He looks like he fits there, in between those two other powerful men.

I'm actually finding his confidence a real turn-on.

I wonder whether he's pissed off that I've found out so much about him in the way I did. Jeff didn't exactly give him a chance to conceal it from us. I can't imagine he'll be *pleased* that I now know something so personal about him. He probably thinks I'll use it against him or something.

My stomach sinks at the thought.

It would be typical, for him to think the worst of me.

'Do you think I should take a position on your father's board?' Jeff suddenly asks me, dragging me out of my twisted thoughts.

I start, then swallow, blink a bit, then finally pull myself together enough to say, 'Yes, err, of course.'

But my pause and stumble must have been too long and too telling because Jeff frowns, as if I've given him a reason to doubt the wisdom of working with my dad.

'Don't bother asking Dee questions like that,' my dad says in an excruciatingly jocular tone, clearly trying to divert Jeff's attention away from me and my faux pas. 'She doesn't have a business head on her. It's Bea you want for those sorts of conversations.'

I'm stunned by his bluntness, but not his attitude. He's always made it very clear I come a distant second to Bea in his estimation.

A familiar rage begins to build inside me.

I see Jem glance round at him, then go to open his mouth to say something. Perhaps to agree with him.

Great, that's all I need.

My ire intensifies.

But I have to keep it under wraps. At least for the time being.

'I thought you said Delilah's a marketing and events manager,' Jeff points out, beating Jem to whatever he was going to say and flashing me an earnest smile. 'I suspect you need some business nous for that kind of role, no?'

I force myself to smile back at him, but keep my mouth shut, just as my dad instructed me to do. *I'm here for my student loan*, I remind myself again. I can take his public disparagement for one day without reacting.

My dad seems to realise he's coming across as a dick and says hastily, 'Yes, yes, of course. I just meant from a C-job level point of view, Bea's your woman. And Jem's your man, of course.'

My fingers fidget in my lap as I push past my nagging anger and force myself to concentrate on the conversation they're all having now, in case they ask for my input again. But, of course, they don't and twenty minutes later, we all finally get to our feet at Jeff's insistence.

'Okay, well, let's take a break and meet for dinner at eight o'clock. I have a few calls to make in the meantime, if you'll excuse me,' he says to my dad.

'Great, see you then,' my dad replies, ushering Jem and me out of the room in front of him.

We walk back down the long tiled corridor to our bedrooms, with Jem and my dad exchanging a few words about the way in which the executive-director role would work with Jeff on board on the way there.

They both ignore me hobbling along behind them.

Which is probably for the best as I'm liable to snap at them right now, judging by how jangled I'm feeling.

When we get to the room, I limp inside and Jem shuts the door behind me without a word.

There's a strange tension in the air, as if he's angry with me.

'Everything okay?' I ask him.

'Yes. Why wouldn't it be?' he says. His tone is abrupt, so I feel sure there's something he's not saying.

Does he think I did a poor job of representing my dad in the meeting?

No, I don't think that could be it. He wouldn't really care about that.

Maybe he's still pissed off about me teasing him about us kissing earlier.

Maybe he's been thinking about it the whole time we were in that meeting.

Like I was.

Heat pools between my thighs and my breath catches in my throat.

Ugh. The last thing I need is to develop a crush on bloody *Jem*. Especially when he thinks so little of me.

'I didn't know that about your dad dying while you were at university,' I blurt, desperately trying to turn my thoughts away from how alone we are in here together.

He turns to look at me and pinches his brows into a frown. 'Bea didn't tell you?'

'No. Believe it or not, we don't sit around discussing the ins and outs of your private life,' I say, trying to keep my tone light and jokey, but totally failing to hit the mark.

'I wasn't suggesting you did,' Jem retorts, sounding offended.

'It's impressive – the way you cared for your parents. I don't know if I'd have been able to do it.'

He looks at me for a second, his gaze hooded, then shrugs. 'You do what you have to do. Anyway' – he waves a dismissive hand – 'I don't really want to talk about that right now.'

'No. Sure,' I say, chastened. I guess it's too personal a thing. Though it wasn't me who asked the initial question of him, it was Jeff, I remind myself. I was just an innocent bystander.

'Where's your mum at the moment?' I ask, not able to stop myself from continuing to pry.

'In an assisted-living complex for people with dementia,' he says, not looking at me, but going to pour himself a glass of water.

'Oh. Right.'

I don't know what else to say. *Sorry* seems so glib.

'Does she know you're here? With me?'

He stills and there's a heavy pause before he says, 'I told her I was coming to Greece, but she probably won't remember. She doesn't even recognise me as her son sometimes.' He drinks the whole glass of water in one go. 'Anyway, like I said, I really don't want to talk about my parents right now, okay?' He turns to give me an *I'm serious* stare.

I nod in agreement.

Of course, I'm not going to push the subject if he doesn't want to talk about it.

Before he went all prickly on me, I was thinking how much I'd still like to give him a hug, but instinctively, I know he'd only reject me again if I tried.

So instead, I sit on the bed and start scrolling through one of my social-media apps on my phone.

He's pretty much ignoring me now while he unpacks his bag and meticulously puts away the meagre number of business-ready clothes he's brought.

'Why bother unpacking?' I say irritably. I'm not sure what's made me so cross but my whole body feels jumpy and adrenal-

ized. 'There's no point. It's a waste of energy when we're going to be leaving tomorrow.'

'Because I like to wear uncrumpled clothes,' he says in a lofty tone.

As if he's only just tolerating how shambolic I am – how much of a *nuisance*.

What's his bloody problem? Why does he have to be so uptight? Keeping himself to himself and not letting anyone get close to him.

I'm sure plenty of women have tried and failed before me, I tell myself.

Not that I have any interest whatsoever in his sex life.

Not one bit.

'I'm going for a bath,' I say, getting up off the bed and limping into the bathroom. I need some time away from him now or I'm going to scream. There's a pressure in my chest that won't go away and I think the only thing that'll help right now is a soothing soak.

The bath is enormous, of course, and it takes quite a while for it to fill, so I sit on the side in my underwear, reading nonsense on my phone, waiting until it gets to about half-full.

Glancing at the level of the water, I notice now that there are lots of little nozzles around the inside of the bath.

Ha! It's one of those ones that turns into a hot tub.

Looking around the edge of the bath, I see a small panel with three buttons on it. It's not entirely obvious which of them do what, so I just jab at one at random to see what happens.

It turns lights on in the bath, which oscillate between all the colours of the rainbow.

Wild.

I press the next one and it turns the light to a soft white, which slowly pulses on and off every few seconds, plunging the bathroom into darkness before re-illuminating.

The final button I press turns the jets on.

Unfortunately, what I don't consider is that the bath is still only half-full, so instead of making bubbles under the water, it blows air just under the surface. This has the effect of turning it into a stream of spray, which hits the side of the bath then fires up into the air like a geyser, soaking me from head to toe. There's so much water spraying into my face, I can't see the buttons to turn them off any more and I shriek in alarm and shout, 'Bloody hell!', terrified I'm going to flood the whole bathroom.

There's a yell of concern from outside, then Jem bursts in through the door, saying, 'What's wrong? Are you okay?' in a panicked voice.

'I can't see to turn it off!' I shout back through the waterfall between us.

He's strides into the room, using his hand to shield his face, and looks around for the controls. But of course, he can't see a thing either.

'For fuck's sake, Dee! Where's the button?'

I pull myself together and blindly feel my way over to the panel on the bath and jab at the controls until the jets stop. Then for good measure, I turn off the taps too.

There's a deathly silence as we turn to look at each other.

I'm soaked to my skin, standing there in my underwear, which has to be completely see-through now.

Jem is also soaked and the white cotton t-shirt and jersey shorts he's changed into while I've been in here stick to his body like a second skin. I can clearly see the shape of his muscles through the material and I swallow hard, my body suddenly all hot and needy.

'Jesus, you're a walking disaster!' he says, tearing his gaze away from my semi-naked body and swiping his hands over his wet face.

'That's a bit bloody rude!' I hiss back, fed up with him being so judgemental. 'It was an accident. It could have happened to anyone.'

'No, Dee, it couldn't. It's only you that attracts such chaos.' His jaw is set and a small muscle is twitching in it, like he's trying to control his frustration with me.

'Why do you hate me so much?' I blurt, hurt welling in my gut.

'Don't be ridiculous. I don't hate you.' But he's not looking at me, he's staring at the wall behind my head.

'Well, it feels like it some days.'

His gaze snaps to mine. 'I don't like the way you play on Bea's sense of sisterly duty, that's all. It's selfish behaviour.'

'How is it selfish? She likes looking out for me. She likes fixing things.'

'She's got enough on her plate without having to mother you.'

'Yeah, well, I never asked her to.'

He drags his gaze away again, this time looking down at the half-full bath. 'Maybe it's time you started looking after yourself,' he grinds out, clearly irritated with me for answering back with the truth.

Bloody Jem, always sitting on his high horse. He doesn't understand what it's like to have a family like mine, always pointing out my flaws, telling me I'm not doing a good enough job – of anything.

'I can look after myself just fine,' I spit. 'I'm not a child.'

'Well, you act like one sometimes!' Jem shouts back, turning to glare at me.

We're both angry now. Furious with each other.

I'm not sure where this rage has come from, but it's positively buzzing in the air between us.

We're only a couple of feet apart but the distance feels enormous.

His gaze flicks downwards for a second, then back up to my face, his scowl deepening.

'Are you checking out my tits?' I scoff, needing an outlet for my frustration.

Colour appears on his cheeks and his jaw tightens.

Ha. So that's it. He doesn't want to be caught ogling me in my see-through underwear. I on the other hand have no compunction whatsoever about checking out the lean contours of his body, which are fully apparent under his soaked clothes.

I drop my gaze to look at him from head to toe, feeling an excited flutter in my chest and an even more excited pressure between my thighs.

The guy has an incredible body.

My fingers itch to touch him.

Looking back into his eyes, they appear dark and hooded, as if he's thinking the exact same thing.

Can that be right?

'Go on then, cop a feel,' I say to him. 'I can tell you want to.'

He appears to freeze.

'Go ahead,' I insist. 'I don't mind.'

I have a ridiculous urge to get some sort of power over him and this seems like the perfect opportunity. Plus, I really would love for him to touch me right now and satisfy this nagging need.

But he doesn't move.

So I take an unsteady step towards him.

He takes a step back.

I take half a one forwards.

After a second's pause, he takes another one backwards, so that now his back is against the wall.

But he doesn't leave.

Reaching towards him, I gently place the flat of my hand on his chest.

'I can feel your heart racing,' I murmur, gazing into his eyes, which look almost black now, his pupils wide and fixed. 'Are you really that angry with me?'

I see him swallow before he says, 'No. Not angry.' His voice is low and rough.

My mouth twitches up in the corner as I feel a surge of pleasure at the way he's reacting to me.

I want this attention from him. I crave it.

But to my frustration, he lifts his hand and prises my fingers away from his chest, forcing my arm down to his side so I can't move it now.

So I put my other hand on his chest instead.

He lifts this one off too, bringing it to his other side.

I'm trapped now, both hands held down by his hips. But it's brought our bodies closer, so there are only a few inches between my mouth and his.

'I don't feel anything for you,' he says.

But I know it's a lie. I can see it in his eyes.

I rock my pelvis forwards, so our bodies are pressed together at the hip. And *yes.*

He's hard.

Like I knew he would be.

Like I *hoped* he would be.

'If you say so,' I say, raising one eyebrow at him – in exactly the way he usually does to me.

His fresh, minty scent tickles my senses. He always smells like this, clean and delicious.

My lust intensifies, rushing the blood through my veins and making my body throb with need.

We stare at each other, locked in a stand-off. Who's going to break it first, either by walking away, or taking it further?

My heart races as I wait to see what his next move will be.

This is one of those moments where life turns on an axis.

Which way will it go?

I know which way I hope it'll spin.

Even though I'm primed for it happening, I'm not prepared for the rush of energy that sweeps through my entire body as he lets out a low breath of frustration and closes the small space between us, covering my mouth with his.

And it's not just a peck. It's a full-on, possessive kiss.

I react instinctively to it, opening my mouth and returning the pressure – kissing him in the way I'd wanted to when I was high the other day.

But I'm not high now.

Not in that way, anyway.

It's rough and messy, this kiss – our teeth clashing and our mouths wet.

Because we're still locked in a fight, I realise.

And it's so damn hot.

I dart my tongue into his mouth and he pulls back from me, though only a few centimetres, as if this added intimacy has made him think he should stop this now, but he isn't entirely convinced he wants to.

I know I don't want him to.

He's still holding on to my wrists and I lift my arms so he has to raise his too, then I guide his hands towards my chest.

He resists for one agonising moment, then gives in to my urging and lets go of my wrists so he can cup both breasts, his fingertips pressing into the soft material of my bra so I can feel the pressure of his touch through it. When he rubs his thumbs over my hard nipples, even though they're covered by the cotton, they're so sensitive, desire barrels through me.

We breathe hard against each other's mouths, our lips close but not quite touching now. He's staring into my eyes, like he's in a trance.

I'm aware of my heart racing and guess he must be able to feel it too, as his thumbs continue to stroke over my nipples.

And then his lips are on mine again, his tongue deep in my mouth. It's urgent and so very deliberate. Like he's given in to something he was fighting.

The idea of this is so exciting, a low moan builds in my throat.

I want more. More kisses. More touching. More of his soft skin over hard muscles under my fingertips.

I press one hand against the wall behind him for balance and stroke the other down his chest to the top of his shorts, enjoying the feel of the ridges of his muscles through the damp t-shirt. I pause for a moment at the waistband of his shorts, giving him time to stop me from going further, but when he doesn't, I slip my hand under the elastic, first of the shorts, then of his boxers.

He sucks in a sharp breath against my mouth, then lets out a low groan of pleasure as my fingertips find the head of his cock.

I wrap my hand around it and move it slowly from tip to base, exploring the length of him.

He's big. Not scarily big, but there's some impressive girth there.

I imagine what it would feel like to have his cock inside me, stretching me and thrusting deep, and my body floods with excitement, triggering a low, determined throb in my pussy.

Moving my hand slowly up his shaft again, I rub my thumb over the head, finding it's slippery with pre-cum. So this is definitely doing it for him too.

I slide my hand slowly down again, then repeat the last motion, drawing another groan from him. I have him pinned to the wall like this and it's brilliantly enabling.

We both know he could easily stop this by pushing me away from him – he's a lot stronger than me after all, in every sense – but he's choosing not to.

His enthusiastic response drives me on. I want to make him groan like that again.

So I keep moving my hand, up and down, up and down, speeding up a little as he starts to jerk his hips.

'Whoa, Dee, whoa, slow down, slow down,' he begs against my mouth, his breath rushing out of him.

But I'm enjoying myself so much, I don't want to slow down and I definitely don't want to stop. I want to see this to its conclusion.

I'm in charge here for once and it feels bloody fantastic.

And then he comes.

Hard.

His entire body jerks against me, and his hands, which are still on my breasts, grip them firmly, like he's trying to anchor himself to me. His lips are still pressed to mine and he moans his pleasure into my mouth, his breath clouding my face, his eyes screwed shut.

It's the sexiest thing I've ever experienced – Jem letting go like this. In front of me. It's such a rush.

The build-up to this has been pretty intense, to be fair, so it's not a surprise he came so quickly.

And I don't care. In fact, I like it. I like that I made this happen. That he had no choice but to let go. Especially because he's been fighting it.

There's something really empowering about that.

His grip on me lessens a little, then his ragged breathing

starts to slow and he moves his hands away from me and rocks his head back till it touches the wall.

'Oh fuck.'

He still has his eyes screwed shut and he's not touching me at all.

I give a little shiver as I feel a distance grow between us again.

What's going on? He can't be regretting this already. Can he?

'Are you okay?' I ask, a little tremulously.

There's a few seconds pause before he opens his eyes and drops his chin to look at me.

'Uh, yeah. I guess. I wasn't... uh, intending that to happen, that's all.'

I'm surprised by how flustered he is.

'You're acting like you've never had a handjob before,' I joke, disconcerted by the extremity of his reaction.

There's a loaded pause where he looks away and refuses to meet my eye.

'I haven't,' he says eventually.

'You've never had a handjob?' I say, incredulous. 'What kind of women are you dating? That's very lax of them.'

'No kind of women.'

'Oh.' It suddenly occurs to me that I've been very presumptuous. 'Men then?'

'No. No kind of men either.'

'So, hang on. Are you telling me you don't date?'

'Yes.'

'Ever?'

'No.'

'So, what, you're a virgin?'

'Can we not...'

I blink at him, completely flummoxed. I never would have

guessed he's never had sex. He's too virile, too, well, *sexy* for that to be believable.

I wonder what's got in the way of that happening.

An unsettling thought strikes me.

'Are you saving yourself for my sister?' I blurt. I realise as soon as I've said it that I don't actually want to hear the answer to that. Especially if I'm right.

'I don't want to talk about Bea right now. Especially after... what just happened here,' he mutters, pushing himself away from the wall and past me.

I take a stumbling step backwards as his movement unbalances me and I have to reach out to steady myself.

'Could you give me the room for a minute please,' he says. But it's not a request, it's a demand.

I nod, my stomach sinking, and grab a towel from the heated rail, which I wrap around myself, then hobble past him and out of the room, hearing him close the door firmly behind me.

I make it over to the bed on shaky legs and flop down onto the mattress, screwing my eyes shut and frowning hard.

I feel weird. Uncomfortable. Like I've done something wrong.

But I haven't, I remind myself. He could have stopped it at any point. I wasn't exactly holding him hostage in there. He was free to leave. He could have said no.

I swallow past a lump in my throat. But then I did push very hard for what I wanted to happen there. Perhaps he didn't feel he *could* say no.

But that's ridiculous, isn't it?

He was turned on. He kissed me first!

I guess as soon as he came down from his horn, he regretted what we'd done immediately.

Especially as I stupidly mentioned Bea.

Ugh!

There's the sound of the bathroom door opening and Jem walks out. His hair looks rumpled, like he's run his fingers through it in agitation, and he's not smiling. He does, at least, look at me.

I sit up as he approaches the bed and swing my legs over the side.

'Bathroom's all yours,' he says.

'Jem? Perhaps we should talk about what just happened?' I say, worried now by the closed expression on his face.

'I'd rather not. It wasn't a good idea and it's not something we should repeat. It'll fuck everything up,' he says, his voice hard, like he's built back his emotional wall between us.

My body rushes with a sickly sort of horror.

'So that's it? We just pretend it didn't happen?' I say. I can hear the frustration in my voice. I don't want to just sweep this under the carpet. It'll be even more difficult being around him from now on if we don't address this right now.

'Yes,' is his determined reply.

I feel emotion closing my throat and I'm suddenly terrified I'm going to cry in front of him.

But I won't give him the satisfaction of seeing that.

'Okay. Fine. Let's forget it happened then,' I say, leaping up from the bed. 'I'm going to have that bath if you're really not prepared to be a grown-up and talk about this.'

He sits down on the bed with his back to me and I see the tension in his shoulders. 'You do that,' is all he says.

I give him another few seconds to come to his senses and at least look at me. But when he doesn't, I let out a low, wobbly sigh and hobble back to the bathroom.

Maybe once we've both had a little while to get our heads

around what happened in here, we'll be able to at least laugh about it, I tell myself.

But I don't really believe that.

And when I come out of the bathroom half an hour later, with my heart in my mouth and my pulse racing, I find the room is empty.

8

JEM

I'm so hacked off with myself.

I can't believe, first of all, that I allowed that to happen. And secondly, that I turned into such a fucking man-child and refused to talk to Dee about it afterwards.

But I was completely freaked out by it.

The sheer force of my need to come had shocked me. I mean, it's human nature to want sex, especially when tensions are running high, like they have been between me and Dee for the last few days, but this felt like something else. Mainly, I think it was a release from the frustration I've been feeling towards her since she fell down those stairs in her bloody high heels and forced everyone to adjust their lives in order to facilitate hers.

But it's not just that.

Sitting there in that meeting with Jeff and seeing how her dad demeaned her suddenly gave me an insight into why she is the way she is. It can't be easy, being treated like you're second best to your own sister, especially when she's as exceptional as Bea.

I felt – not *sorry* for Dee exactly, but like I understood her a little better, and honestly, it spun me out a bit. It made me feel *unsettled* around her. So much so, I was angry with her when we'd first walked back into the bedroom after the meeting with Jeff. But I wasn't sure why.

I was already hyped up, I guess, after all the crazy goings-on from the last couple of days, on top of her little skit about trying to kiss me earlier, that had made me vibrate with sexual tension. It had hung about, flaring up in my mind every few minutes, all throughout the meeting. Perhaps it had been all of that coming to a head.

And then, of course, when I'd run into the bathroom after hearing her shout, my blood had been up in expectation of finding she'd hurt herself, but instead I got a full-frontal vision of her in just her underwear. Her soaked underwear. Which may as well have not been there. She has an incredible body: soft and curvy, but strong from exercise. And she is, like her sister, a beautiful woman. But she has a different energy to Bea. A sexier energy.

A more dangerous energy.

The memory of her jerking me off, her hot, soft mouth on mine, plays on repeat in my head as I stride around the gardens outside, trying to walk off my agitation, but to my utter frustration, I'm getting hard again at the thought of it instead.

Clearly my body wants more of what just took place in that bathroom.

But this doesn't mean I should get sexually involved with her. As much as my cock might be telling me I should right now.

With any luck, Tim will conclude his business here with Jeff by tomorrow and we'll be on our way home before the end of the day and I won't have to see Dee much, if at all, once we're back in Bath. But we still need to get through dinner this evening and sleep in the same room together afterwards.

Stepping back into the house, I walk around the ground floor, pacing from room to room, still trying to straighten myself out. Luckily, there doesn't seem to be anyone else about.

There's the distant clinking of dinner being prepared coming from a kitchen on the other side of the house though, so I'm not going to go anywhere near that. I need quiet and time on my own right now.

I should pull myself together and enjoy being here, on a *private island*, for God's sake.

Strolling over to a black lacquered grand piano in the corner of the living room, I peer at the silver-framed photos arranged on the shiny lid. There's one of Jeff and an attractive black-haired woman, who looks to be around the same age as him in the picture. I'm guessing it's his wife, or partner, because they're leaning towards each other with their arms entwined, and their body language looks loving and comfortable. The photo next to it is older, because the two of them are more youthful looking. And there's a young black-haired man in-between them in this one. He looks a lot like the woman in the picture, so I'm guessing he's their son. Tim didn't mention that Jeff has a son in the short, terse briefing he gave Dee and me on the journey here.

I'll have to ask Jeff about him later.

Speaking of which, I really should get back to the room and dress for dinner.

Which means seeing and talking to Dee.

How am I going to handle this? She didn't seem at all fazed by the incident in the bathroom, until I closed down on her that is, so I get the impression she'd be perfectly happy to let something more develop between us.

Goddamn it.

How did things suddenly get so messed up?

I can't let myself get any more emotionally involved with her than I already am. I'd be crazy to. We're so very badly matched and it would be an absolute disaster to let anything else happen.

I really don't have capacity in my life right now to take on someone as demanding as Dee.

Granted, it may not be a great idea for Bea and me to be together as a couple right now either, when we're just starting our business, but I'm hoping there might be an opportunity to explore it as an option in the future when we're both in the position to.

That's not going to happen if this thing with Dee gets in the way, though.

I need to be very firm that nothing else is going to develop between us. I'll play at being her partner and do whatever's necessary to pull it off in front of Jeff and her dad, but that's all.

With that fortifying thought in mind, I walk slowly back to the bedroom and take a calming breath before opening the door.

She's not here.

I check the bathroom.

Nope. Not there either. Just the residual steam from her bath.

Where did she go?

Now I've decided to talk to her about this, I'm annoyed that she's not here.

My nerves are jumping.

Okay. No problem. We can talk later.

I change into smart trousers and a loose cotton shirt for dinner, in deference to our host, then I leave the room again and go for another wander outside to walk off my agitation.

It's not cold out here, but there's a portentous feeling in the air. Dark clouds are building in the distance and even as I watch them, they seem to be moving gradually closer to us here on the island. We weren't warned there was going to be a storm, but I know from experience that weather patterns can suddenly take a turn for the worse. I did a weekend of hiking for my Duke of Edinburgh during my GCSEs and even though it had been predicted to be sunny for the whole time we were there, a sudden torrential rainstorm had caught us off guard on the second day.

Even the inside of our boots were soaked.

Not fun.

And while storms might be beautiful to look at and can be exciting to experience, they're also dangerous to be caught in the middle of. This one has the potential to cause some major disruption.

I do *not* want to be stuck here any longer than necessary. I'm already deeply regretting saying I'd come in the first place.

But I'm doing it for Bea, I remind myself. I don't want her to have to worry about what's going on with her sister and dad while she's at the hotel.

And meeting Jeff has been a blast too. I'm fascinated by anyone that can achieve that level of success – especially someone who's come from humble beginnings. It gives me hope.

I make my way through the manicured gardens to a viewpoint that looks out across the island and out over the Aegean Sea. How incredible it must feel to own an actual island. Especially one as cool as this. I experience another rush of awe towards Jeff. Maybe, if I play things right, one day my own business ventures will be as successful as his and I'll end up hanging out in the same social sphere as people like him. Wouldn't that be wild.

'Excuse me, sir,' a deep, male voice says behind me, making me jump.

I turn to see a tall guy in tan-coloured chinos and a white shirt walking towards me from the house. It's Jeff's sort-of butler. He looks like he might be a Greek native, though I have to admit, I'm not the best at guessing people's nationalities. I'd say he's in his late-twenties and is striking-looking, with dark, deep-set eyes and a strong jawline.

I imagine he's exactly the sort of guy Dee would go gaga over.

I force down a weird prickling sort of irritation. Who Dee finds attractive should be – and is – of absolutely no interest to me.

'Yes?' I say to him.

'Drinks are being served on the terrace if you'd like to join everyone else before dinner.'

'Oh. Right, yeah. Okay,' I say, giving the guy a nod, trying not to look panicked at being found wandering on my own when I should have been with Dee.

'It's this way,' he says, sweeping his hand towards the house and setting off in that direction.

I follow him, jogging to catch him up before we get to the terrace on the other side of the house, not wanting to appear to be lagging in his wake.

Tim, Jeff and Dee are all already here, drinks in hand. The men have glasses of wine and as I turn to look at Dee, I see she has one too. I'm surprised. I would have thought she'd have gone for a beer or even a cocktail. Wine doesn't seem like her, some-how. Too refined, maybe. Or too stuffy.

I guess she's just trying to fit in to please her dad.

I experience another sting of annoyance on her behalf towards Tim and his earlier belittling behaviour.

'Ah, Jem. Come and join us,' Tim calls as I walk towards the wrought-iron table where they're all sitting.

After a moment's hesitation, I take a chair next to Dee, figuring it would be expected for me to sit with her, as her partner.

I catch her scent in the air as I sit down, and I'm glad we're sitting at a table so no one will notice my immediate physical reaction to it.

What the hell's going on with my body? It's like she's unleashed something that's been lying dormant up till now.

She doesn't turn to look at or acknowledge me, so I throw myself into chatting with Tim and Jeff about the economy.

Every now and again, I'm aware of Dee shifting in her seat next to me, which has the effect of distracting me for a few seconds so I keep losing the thread of the conversation.

Finally, the guy in the chinos comes back to the table to let us know that the evening meal is being served in the dining room.

We all get up from the table and follow him into the house, with Tim walking with Jeff, leaving Dee and me to follow them.

Just before we go in through the doorway, I touch her arm to get her attention.

'Hey. Look, sorry for running out on you. Let's talk later, okay? After dinner?'

The look she gives me is initially devoid of any expression, but I catch a flash of hurt in her eyes. 'Don't worry about it. There's nothing to talk about,' she says, before pushing past me and walking into the house after the two men.

I stare after her, my stomach sinking.

Shit.

I should have gone back sooner, so we could have thrashed this thing out between us before we were stuck together at dinner.

But it's too late for that now. I'm just going to have to get through this evening without our animosity towards each other showing and giving Jeff any reason to doubt we're a solid couple. I'd hate to put Tim's mission here in jeopardy. I need him on my side. He'll make a powerful ally but a formidable opponent if he thinks I'm in any way responsible for messing with his business objectives.

As I predicted, Dee makes a show of being especially friendly towards the chinos guy as he serves us our dinner of grilled fish and Mediterranean vegetables.

So much so that I feel I have to lean towards her during the meal, when Jeff and Tim are deep in discussion about the last election, and whisper, 'Jeff's going to get suspicious about us not being a couple if you keep flirting with that guy.'

Dee turns to me, her eyes wide with incredulity, and whispers back, 'Well, then you need to pretend to find me more attractive, don't you.'

I swallow hard. Clearly, she's still in a funk about me legging it earlier and she's not going to make this evening easy for either of us.

Out of the corner of my eye, I see Tim shoot us a look, as if he's becoming aware of the atmosphere between the two of us and is warning us to pull ourselves together.

So, I do the only thing I can think of and move one hand under the table to grip the top of her thigh, then cup her jaw with the other and lean forwards to kiss her gently on the mouth, trying to put as much affection into the action as I can for our audience and hoping to God she won't reject me publicly.

I feel her stiffen for a second under my touch, before she gives in to me and relaxes, returning the pressure on my mouth.

When I draw back, I smile at her, then slide my hands away from her body and turn back to my meal, aware of Tim returning to his conversation with Jeff, seemingly satisfied there's nothing amiss here. Dee, however, is staring at the side of my head in what I think must be surprise.

Thank God she doesn't have her hand on my thigh, or she'd

know exactly how much that kiss affected me. I don't want her thinking it was anything but an act for Jeff and her dad.

We manage to get through the rest of dinner without further incident, with Dee even joining in on the conversation about the best eco alternatives to fossil fuels.

Jeff encourages her to talk and her body language visibly relaxes as she's given the space to voice her views.

It strikes me that perhaps this isn't the norm when her dad is around.

In fact, the more time I'm spending around her, the clearer it's becoming that Tim's style of parenting has a lot to answer for. I guess it's been okay for Bea because she's interested in the same kind of things he is, but Dee is another story altogether.

And, if I'm honest, I have to admit, it's a story I'm becoming more and more invested in.

9

DELILAH

So, dinner started in the most awkward of ways, with Jem turning up late to drinks on the terrace and then basically ignoring me – as usual. As if that handjob in the bathroom hadn't even happened.

It didn't feel great, I have to say.

I'm aware that I've been uncharacteristically quiet during the meal too, but honestly, it's almost impossible to get a word in with the three of them jabbering away, and I know my dad will probably railroad me into silence anyway, since he won't trust me not to show him up in some way again.

Jem seems impervious to my mood too.

So I'm totally stunned when he leans over and kisses me, right there at the table.

I'm sure he's only doing it for show in front of Jeff and my dad, since we must be giving out visibly hostile vibes, but even so.

It takes me right back to the kiss in the bathroom and it's all I can do to sit still and ignore the pulsing sexual need that builds between my thighs as I desperately try to concentrate on the conversation about alternatives to fossil fuels that Jeff kindly includes me in.

Bloody Jem seems completely unfazed by the tension between us and carries on eating as if nothing untoward just happened.

How can he be so insensitive?

There's a short pause in the conversation where the hot Greek guy in chinos – Nico, I think Jeff called him – who's been serving us comes to clear the table. I've only been extra friendly towards him because he's the only one actually giving me any real attention right now. I guess Jem's right, though; I should probably rein it in so as not to look suspect in front of Jeff.

Whilst Nico tops up our wine glasses, Jem takes the opportunity of the interruption to grill Jeff about his own family.

'I noticed some photos on the piano,' he says. 'Is it your wife and son in them with you?'

A sad smile passes over Jeff's face and out of the corner of my eye, I see my father stiffen.

Jeff doesn't seem to mind the question though, because he sits back in his seat and gives a nod. 'Yes, my late wife and son.'

'Oh, I'm so sorry,' Jem says.

I glance at him and see he has a stricken look on his face.

At least it's not just me making conversational faux pas today.

'My wife died a few years ago of cancer, but we lost my son when he was twenty-four. He was such a bright kid. Kind, charismatic and very funny. He'd make my wife and me laugh all the time. I miss him a lot.'

'I bet you do,' Jem says, his voice filled with sympathy.

'You remind me of him, actually,' Jeff says, giving Jem a warm smile now. 'You have a similar sort of energy.'

'Well, I take that as a huge compliment, sir, thank you,' Jem says.

Nico reappears and leans in to speak quietly, but urgently, into Jeff's ear. His body language looks a little tense too and the rest of us glance at each other, wondering what the cause for alarm is.

The minute Nico walks away, Jeff turns to us with a rueful expression. 'Apologies for this, but I'm told I need to leave the island tonight as there's some bad weather approaching Greece, which might delay my flight out to Tanzania tomorrow. I don't want to inconvenience the group I'm climbing Kilimanjaro with, so forgive me if I cut our time together here short.'

He turns to fix my dad with his intent gaze now and says, 'Well, Tim, I think we can do business. Consider me in. But let's dot the i's etcetera once I'm back from my climb.'

My dad frowns at this, clearly not wanting to leave things hanging, I guess in case Jeff changes his mind in the meantime.

But before he can open his mouth, Jeff turns to address Jem.

'Listen, son. If things don't work out for any reason with your current business, give me a call, okay. I'll happily find you a position in my London office. I like to give people with drive and determination like yours opportunities they might not ordinarily have and I think we'd work well together.'

'Uh, yes, okay,' Jem says, clearly taken aback by this direct offer. 'Thank you. I'll keep it in mind.'

'You do that.'

Jeff then turns to fix me with his warm, kindly gaze. 'Great to meet you, Delilah. It's been a real pleasure spending time with you. I have to say, you and Jem make a delightful couple. I applaud your choice in partner. Don't let this guy go, okay? I can tell he's going far. And believe me, I know what I'm talking about.'

I'm stunned. The Great Sir Jeff Blackmore seems to genuinely think I deserve someone as set for greatness as Jem in my life.

I'm horrified to feel tears pool in my eyes.

Blinking them away quickly, I shoot Jeff a quick smile then stare down at my hands in my lap, hoping to God someone else will take the conversational lead so I can have a minute to pull myself together.

Once again, it's my dad that steps in.

'Listen, Jeff. Can I catch a ride back in the chopper with you now? I'd like to pick your brain about a couple of things, now you're on board with, er, being on my board.'

There's a small pause before Jeff says, 'Sure. That'll work. I'm afraid I can't take all of you back tonight, though. The helicopter can only take three passengers.'

'No problem,' my father says before anyone else can say anything. 'I'm sure Jem and Dee won't mind flying out in the morning instead.'

Jeff nods. 'Okay. I'll send the helicopter back for the two of you tomorrow. I can't ask him to fly back again tonight, I'm afraid. Rules and regulations about flight hours.'

There's a tense silence before my dad jumps in again. 'No problem at all. You don't mind staying and flying tomorrow, right?' He gives Jem and me both a look that says, *Don't you dare disagree.*

So we both duly nod.

'Sure. We're happy to stay the night here, if that's okay with you, Jeff?' Jem says.

'Of course,' Jeff says, getting up from his chair and walking over to slap Jem gently on the back. 'You two enjoy yourselves. You're welcome to stay for longer, if you'd like.'

'No, no,' Jem says quickly. A little too quickly for my liking.

But Jeff doesn't seem to notice. 'Okay, well, if you'll excuse me, I need to make a couple of calls before we head out.' He turns to my dad. 'See you out at the helipad in twenty.'

He strides towards the door, leaving the three of us still sitting there. Turning back at the last minute, he gives us a salute and says, 'Great spending time with you,' before vacating the room.

As soon as he's out of sight, my dad sits back in his chair with a satisfied sigh. 'Good. Well done, both of you. He's in.' He slaps his hands onto the table in glee. I don't think I've ever seen him so happy.

I, on the other hand, am not exactly delighted about the sudden turn of events.

'I can't believe you're just running out and leaving us here,' I say, trying to keep my exasperation out of my voice, but failing spectacularly.

'You'll both be fine here for one night,' my dad says blithely, waving away my comment as if it means nothing to him. 'I'd have thought you'd want to make the most of staying here a bit longer, anyway.'

'Well, I don't. I have a job to get back to, remember.'

My dad lets out a disparaging snort. 'It doesn't sound like that place is going to survive from what you've told me. And forgive me, Delilah, but I'm not sure you have the skillset to turn around the fortunes of a failing hotel.'

The hard pressure in my throat is back, but it's my rage that wins out. 'I don't appreciate you speaking to me like I'm your incompetent employee! I'm your daughter. Who you're supposed to love and support,' I hiss at him.

My dad folds his arms and stares me down. 'Look, Delilah, I'm sorry but you have no idea how much effort and bloody-minded determination it takes to run a successful business. You constantly have people snapping at your heels trying to steal your customers or take you down. It's cut-throat and you have to be bullish and take every opportunity you're offered. I am how I am because I have to be. You can't just sit back and faff about with arty pursuits and expect success to come to you. You have to throw everything at it to make it happen and I don't see you doing that.'

'Yeah, but at what cost, Dad? Your marriage? All the other relationships in your life?'

My dad lets out a frustrated growl and snaps, 'You're being naïve. You're just like your bloody mother. And I don't have time for this.'

He stands up from the table and starts to walk away from us.

'No. Right. You never have time for me. It's always business first,' I call after him.

But he doesn't even turn around to acknowledge me. He's made up his mind and the rest of us can lump it.

I let out my own growl of frustration, then turn to glance at Jem, who's been watching this whole embarrassing debacle in silence.

He goes to open his mouth to say something, but I don't want to hear it. I don't need his sage opinion right now.

'I'm going back to the room,' I say, struggling up from my chair and limping away from him as fast as I can.

The last thing I need is a lecture about how my dad is right and I should pull my socks up from Mr Binary-Business-Boffin himself.

'I'll see you later,' I call over my shoulder.

I don't wait for his answer.

10

JEM

I sit at the table for another fifteen minutes, finishing my glass of wine, to give Dee a bit of time on her own.

I can see why she'd be upset after being spoken to like that by her own father and I'm not sure what I could say to make her feel better right now.

My skin rushes with a murky sense of discomfort.

What with my less than friendly reaction to the incident in the bathroom earlier, then my misjudged attempt to fix it by kissing her in full public view where she was forced to go along with it, on top of her dad degrading and humiliating her in front of me and Jeff, she's not exactly having a great day.

And I feel shitty for being partly to blame for that.

Dee isn't a mean person. She can be infuriating and a little selfish sometimes, but the more I get to know her, the more I get why.

Her self-esteem has clearly taken some severe knocks in the past and she's drawn a protective cloak around herself, using humour and what comes across as self-centred nonchalance to maintain her composure.

It was actually quite a turn-on to see her standing up for herself at the table just now.

She's definitely got some balls and, it seems, is actually more like her dad than I gave her credit for.

I like that.

When I get back to the room, I find her sitting on the bed with her knees drawn up to her chin and her arms wrapped around her shins.

'Hey,' I say, walking over and sitting on the edge of the bed.

'Hey,' she says, her voice flat. 'Well, that was the most intense dinner I've ever had.'

'Yeah,' I agree. 'Are you okay? Your dad was being a bit of a dick there at the end.'

'You think?' she says, loading her tone with sarcasm. She lets out a heavy sigh and flaps her hand at me, but doesn't meet my eye. 'But, yeah, I'm fine. It's all just par for the course with me and my dad.'

There's an uncomfortable pause.

'Do you want to talk about it?'

'Not really.'

'Sure?'

'I'm fine,' she says, sounding a bit frustrated now. 'You don't need to coddle me.'

She's closed down on me, the way I closed down on her earlier.

It feels really crap.

'Look, I *am* sorry about the way I acted earlier,' I say.

Unwrapping her arms from around her legs, she shoots me a tight smile, then gets off the bed. 'You don't need to apologise again. It's okay. Really. I get it. It was a moment of madness, like you said. No harm done.'

I watch as she hobbles towards the bathroom and shuts the

door, not giving me a chance to respond to that. Not that there's any response I can give other than, *Okay, good.*

This doesn't feel good, though.

I wait, sitting on the bed, till she emerges again in her pjs, her face free of the make-up she was wearing at dinner, looking more vulnerable and younger than I've ever seen her.

Something twists in my chest.

'Bathroom's free,' she says, waving her hand towards it, but not looking directly at me as she moves to the other side of the bed from where I'm sitting.

'Okay, thanks,' I say. I guess we're done with conversation now then. Maybe it's for the best.

I get up and go into the bathroom, taking my time getting washed and dressed into my sleep shorts. When I come out, Dee's already in bed, under the duvet, with the light out.

Trying not to make any noise and disturb her, I lie down on the sofa and pull the eiderdown that I took off the bed earlier to use as a cover over myself.

Once I've settled in, I lie there, listening to the sound of the wind outside. It's definitely got up since we were in the garden earlier and is making a hollow, howling sort of noise as it batters the walls of the house. A bit like a low wail. It's a little unsettling. But I'm sure Jeff wouldn't have left us here if he thought we'd be in any danger. This house will have been pummelled by a lot of storms throughout the years he's owned it and it's still standing firm.

Dee turns over in the bed, distracting me from my musings about the weather, and I stare up at the ceiling trying not to think about everything that happened between us today.

But it's no use. It all keeps going round and round my head on a never-ending loop.

I can't stop thinking about how impossible I'd found it to

walk out of the bathroom. How, deep down, I think I'd wanted it to happen. That I'd lost my mind for a while there.

My body rushes again at the memory of how amazing I'd felt in those moments. How buzzed. How *alive*.

Some devilish instinct inside of me wants more, too. But I really shouldn't let myself go there. I'd be crazy to allow it to go any further.

Ugh.

I seem to have opened a portal to hell.

Well, maybe *hell* is a bit strong.

But some kind of purgatory, at least.

Dee turns over again with a frustrated-sounding sigh.

It seems like she's having trouble sleeping too.

After another quarter of an hour of her tossing and turning, I hear her get out of bed, hobble towards the bathroom and quietly close the door.

A few moments later, what sounds like her electric tooth-brush starts up.

The teeth-brushing goes on for quite a while and there's another strange noise accompanying it that sounds a lot like heavy breathing. I listen in fascinated silence, straining to hear, and I'm rewarded with what sounds like a low moan. Then silence.

I turn over awkwardly on the sofa, adjusting my position so my erection isn't pressing into the cushions any more.

Self-conscious heat washes over me.

It's not surprising she needed to get herself off when I didn't make any kind of move to reciprocate what she'd done for me earlier. Not that I'd know exactly what to do. Things have never quite aligned for me when it's come to sex and relationships with women. Not that I haven't wanted it to. In fact, I've been pretty frustrated at points, especially when I've come close but ended up thwarted for one reason or another.

So, as Dee discovered earlier, I'm still pretty green.

I've seen plenty of films with sex in them of course, but I've avoided watching any explicit porn. I've always worried it was exploitative towards women and didn't want to feel I had any part of that. I should probably look up techniques for future reference though, should I need them at some point in the future.

Not with Dee, of course. That would be crazy.

The door clicks open and I freeze, pretending to be asleep, as she limps slowly out of the bathroom and back to her bed.

There's the sound of her shifting around, plumping up the pillow, then pulling the duvet over herself. Then, finally, silence settles over us.

After a few more minutes, I hear her breathing slowing down and becoming more regular, as if she's fallen asleep now.

I'm too wired to sleep, so I spend a while looking up the best techniques for making women orgasm on my phone. Huh. I had no idea there were so many different things to consider. It's actually quite fascinating.

After I've read my fill of new, mindboggling information, I stare up at the ceiling for what feels like another hour before deciding to do something about the persistent hard-on that now just won't bloody go down.

Carefully, and as quietly as I can, I roll off the sofa and creep over to the bathroom, closing the door behind me, and take Dee's lead, giving my body the release it's been desperate for since the last time I was in here.

Thank God we're leaving tomorrow.

11

DELILAH

I finally managed to sleep once I'd got myself off.

But I wake early the next morning and lie there listening to the whistling of the wind outside. If anything, it sounds more ferocious than it did last night, not less.

Yikes.

I hope the storm's going to pass soon so the helicopter can land safely later.

Shoving my niggling worry about this aside, I turn my thoughts to what happened with Jem yesterday.

My body's been humming with sexual energy ever since he walked away from me after that *mistake* in the bathroom, then gave me that deeply hot kiss at the dinner table in front of Jeff and my dad, where I couldn't do anything but take it. Which had its own kind of erotic power.

And it doesn't seem to have calmed down overnight either.

I'm still really turned on.

The trouble is, now we've opened that door, I want more. Much more. But Jem's made it clear it's not on the cards and – typically – being denied it is only increasing my longing for it.

Frustration doesn't even come close to what I'm feeling right now.

But it's probably only because I've not dated in a while.

So I should put the guy right out of my head.

At least we'll be getting out of here today, and now the swelling on my ankle has started to go down and it feels marginally less painful – to the point where I'm not needing to use the crutches any more – I'll be able to get back to my flat soon and we won't need to be in the same vicinity as each other.

That'll be a relief for both of us, I'm sure.

I hear the sounds of Jem starting to move about on the other side of the room and I peep out over my duvet, to where he's been sleeping on the sofa with the blanket covering his legs.

He's not wearing a t-shirt and I see his muscles flex under his skin as he goes to sit up.

My heart skips.

Dammit! He's not helping matters by hanging out in front of me half naked.

Crossly, I sit up and swing my legs over the side of the bed, then get up unsteadily and make for the bathroom, keeping my gaze front and centre.

'Morning,' Jem says as I limp past him.

'Morning,' I mutter back, my eyes trained hard on the bathroom door.

As soon as I'm in there, I huff out a low, grumpy sigh. This is ridiculous. I can't let him get to me like this. It's Jem, the nerdy virgin we're talking about here... Oh, God. That doesn't help at all. In fact, it makes him seem even sexier. Off limits all the way.

Ack!

I take my time in the shower, trying to ignore how tingly and sensitive my skin feels, but finally give in to the urge and use the pulse of the water between my legs to get some relief. After getting out, I brush my teeth and wrap one of the big fluffy bath sheets around me and exit the bathroom, steeling myself against what else I might see out here. Jem doing push-ups, perhaps, his naked torso gleaming with sweat.

But thankfully – and a little disappointingly if I'm honest – he doesn't appear to be in the room.

Pulling on my clothes quickly, I run a brush through my wet hair, leaving it to dry naturally for the time being, and go to find a strong cup of coffee and some fortifying toast.

I'm ravenous this morning, to the point where my stomach is audibly rumbling.

All that wanking has depleted my reserves.

There's an amazing smell of coffee and bacon and eggs coming from the direction of the dining room.

Following my nose, I limp into the room to find Jem already sitting at the table, eating some poached eggs on toast and chatting with a female member of Jeff's staff, who is also stunning-looking. Does Jeff only surround himself with good-looking people? I guess if I was a billionaire, I might do the same thing, just for kicks.

Ha. As if.

The chances of becoming halfway wealthy as an artist are miniscule, as my dear dad likes to remind me on a regular basis.

Intellectually, I know he's got a point. But I have to at least try to make it as an artist, especially now, while I don't have any dependents. I figure I've got to give it a shot, or I'll always regret it.

'Good morning, Ms Donovan. Would you like some breakfast?' the woman asks me as I approach the table.

I glance at Jem, who looks back at me with one of his trademark eyebrow-raises, and my stomach flips over.

What the hell? Since when did I find that sexy?

Good grief. This is not good.

'Er, yes please,' I say to the woman. 'I'll have a latte and some bacon and scrambled eggs, please.'

She nods. 'Of course. Coming right up. Please take a seat.'

I watch her saunter off and turn to see Jem is doing the same. When he realises I'm looking at him, his gaze snaps to mine.

'How are you this morning?' he asks stiffly.

'Fine. You?'

'Yeah. Okay. Except...' I see him swallow, and colour appears on his cheeks. 'It sounds as if the weather front's moving this way now. They're concerned there might be really strong winds soon so they can't send the helicopter for us this morning.'

'What!' I'm suddenly hot, and dread pools in my stomach. 'So when can they send it?'

'They don't know yet. It depends on what the weather does. I checked the forecasting app and it doesn't look good.'

'What do you mean by *not good*?'

'Dangerously high winds and torrential rain.'

I stare at him. 'You mean a hurricane?'

'Actually, I think they're called *medicanes* over here.'

I frown at him and raise my own eyebrow. It's typical of Jem to know the technical term – and to let me know it. 'All right, Pedantic Man. *Medicane* then.'

Jem just snorts and shakes his head. 'Look, we'll just have to wait it out. Hopefully, it'll pass by quickly. Then they can send the helicopter for us later and we'll fly back to England tonight instead.'

How can he be so calm?

He's probably just fronting it out so he doesn't have to spend the next twenty-four hours with someone who's freaking out.

'What if it doesn't pass quickly?'

'Then we stay here till it's safe to travel.'

I put my head in my hands.

'At least there are worst places to be stuck,' Jem says in a falsely bright voice.

I look up to see him gazing around the grand dining room.

'You think a tiny island in the middle of the Aegean Sea *isn't* the worst place to be trapped during a hurricane – sorry, *medicane*?' I say, intensely aware of the shake in my voice now.

I have to be honest, I'm a bit scared about the idea of being here when it fully hits.

'Alina tells me we'll be perfectly safe here in the house. It's been built to withstand that kind of weather. So don't worry.'

'But I have to get back for my job! What's Bea going to say? She's going to be so pissed off with me.' Adrenaline is ricocheting through my body now, making me twitch. Suddenly, everything seems overwhelming and I feel a primal kind of panic begin to rise from deep inside me.

'Dee? Are you okay?' Jem asks, leaning in towards me and putting his hand on my arm.

I'm only able to suck in stuttering breaths now and I'm worried I'm starting to hyperventilate.

'Hey, it's okay. Just try and slow your breathing,' Jem says in a soothing voice, gently rubbing my arm in comforting strokes.

But it's not helping.

I stare at him in panic. The world seems to have shrunk into a small space around us and it feels as if the air has become too thick and hot to breathe. I'm struggling to drag it into my lungs.

Somewhere in my consciousness, I'm aware of Jem getting up from his seat and the next thing I know, he's lifting me up from my chair and pulling me against him. He wraps his arms around me, then slides one hand into my hair, angling my head against his chest, whilst drawing big, gentle circles onto my back with the other.

'Just breathe, it's okay. I've got you. You'll be okay,' he says in a soothing, calm voice.

I can hear his heart thumping against my ear and I force myself to concentrate on the steady beat of it, trying to match the rhythm of my breathing to his.

The warmth of his body bleeds into mine and the now-familiar scent of him acts as a balm to my fear, quieting my whirling thoughts.

God, it feels so good to be held like this.

So peaceful.

My body gives an involuntary shiver.

It's both wonderful and terrible being this close to him again.

And I know I have to woman the hell up because I really don't want him to see me being this pathetic.

Come on, breathe! Pull yourself together!

With a monumental effort, I draw in a long, steadying breath and gently, but decisively, untangle myself from his embrace.

'I'm okay now,' I say, forcing myself to look at him and move my mouth into a smile.

He frowns at me, clearly not entirely convinced by my shaky statement.

'You sure?'

'Yep.'

'Hmm,' he says.

I hold up both hands in a show of surrender.

'Okay. Yes. I admit it. I, err, freaked out a little bit there,' I say with an embarrassed smile.

'No shit.'

But then he grins at me and the warmth in his eyes hits me right in the chest.

It's this flash of friendly indulgence that finally helps me relax all the way back to where I want to be.

Because of this, I feel like it's going to be okay. We'll be fine if we hunker down together. I trust him on that.

I think.

Though, it's not like I have a choice. We're going to have to ride this thing out and deal with whatever comes at us.

But at least I'm not on my own.

And we have the whole of this amazing house to explore to distract ourselves.

If we manage to find a way to be around each other, we could maybe, *possibly*, have some fun here.

12

JEM

'Hey, do you fancy checking out the rest of the house with me?' I ask Dee, trying not to feel aggrieved at the way she pushed me away, just when I was starting to reconnect with her.

I know it was probably a bit of a liberty, pulling her against me like that, but I acted on instinct. It seemed like the right thing to do in the moment.

Honestly, I don't think I've ever seen her so vulnerable, and it did something to me. Made me want to step up and protect her.

Not that I'm in the market for another person to look after, I remind myself.

'Yeah, sure. I was just about to suggest that myself. Let's get into all the nooks and crannies of this place and see if we can discover its dark underbelly,' Dee says with a wink.

My spirits lift.

It's good to see her back on form.

I've missed it.

Funny that. I'd never have thought I'd miss anything about Dee.

'You're on,' I say, gesturing for her to take the lead.

Pushing away from the table, she makes for the entrance hall. It's positioned in the centre of the house and has a number of doors leading off it in different directions. We already know where the corridor to our room goes, so she ignores that one, instead choosing one opposite the front door. It leads down another long, tiled corridor to a large glass door, through which we can see an indoor pool.

As Dee steps up to the door, it automatically slides to the right with a soft swishing sound, and a blast of warm, faintly chlorinated air hits us.

She turns to look at me and pulls a *what have we got here?* face.

'Do you fancy going for a swim?' I ask her. I know I do. It would be a great way to pass some time. My whole body feels over-energised and I'm craving some hard exercise right now.

'I didn't bring any swimmers,' she says with a rueful grimace.

'Me neither, but I expect the staff can loan us some. If Jeff entertains here a lot, he's probably got spares for guests.'

'True,' Dee says with a slow smile, her eyes lighting up.

My stomach flips at the sight of it. She's so openly expressive when she's happy. It's kind of cool.

'I'll go and ask Alina,' I say, already backing away from her before she notices how I'm reacting to her.

I find Alina in the kitchen with Nico, the butler. They're having a low, murmured conversation in Greek with their backs turned to me, but as soon as I give a discreet cough, she turns to face me and flashes a warm smile.

'Hello. Can I help you with something?' she asks.

'Do you happen to have swimming costumes that Dee and I can borrow?' I ask.

She nods. 'Of course, I'll get them for you. Wait one second, please.'

I watch her walk out, then turn to give Nico a nod of acknowledgement.

He nods back, a faint smile on his lips.

I wonder whether he saw me kissing Dee at the table last night. And whether he knew it was a reaction to her flirting with him.

We wait in uncomfortable silence for Alina to return, both staring out of the kitchen window towards a stunning, but stormy, view across the small island to the now rather rough sea. The trees are waving wildly in the wind that's got up since this morning and a light shower of rain is falling, making the leaves look glossy and vibrantly green. It's nowhere near a *medicane* right now, but there's a definite dark front of clouds moving in, giving the vista an ominous vibe.

Something big and scary is on the way. I just hope it doesn't hit us too hard.

To my relief, Alina reappears a moment later with the costumes in her hand.

At least, I think they're swimming costumes.

My stomach sinks as I take in what she's brought me.

I swear her eyes twinkle as she hands them over. There's a hint of mischief there, I'm sure of it. But all I can say is, 'Thank you,' as I take them from her outstretched hand. I don't want to look like a dick by demanding alternatives, not when they've been looking after us so well. It would feel rude to complain in any way.

'Just leave them in the linen basket in your room once you've finished with them,' she says, widening her smile. 'There are plenty of towels in the changing rooms too.'

I give her a jerky nod. 'Will do.'

I get out of there quickly, my face flaming and my blood up. *Dammit.*

I'm intensely aware of the folly of my suggestion that Dee and I go swimming now as I stride back to the pool. I'm going to have to hang out with her for the next hour or so in just a pair of tiny Speedos whilst trying not to let my body react to the sight of her rocking this scrap of a bikini.

God, I hope she doesn't think I chose these myself.

As soon as I step in through the sliding door to the pool, I see her lying on one of the plush loungers, which are facing the floor-to-ceiling window that looks out over the immaculately manicured garden. Rain is lashing against the glass now and running in rivulets down it, giving the scene a distorted look.

'Did they have any?' Dee calls to me.

'Err, yeah. But I'm not sure they're going to fit,' I say, holding them up for her to see.

A horrified smile breaks across her face. 'You're kidding me!'

'Nope. This is all they had, apparently,' I say, omitting that I felt too uncomfortable to ask Alina for something less revealing.

'Oh. Well. Okay then. Pass mine over and I'll try it on,' Dee says with a slight wobble in her voice.

I walk over and toss the bikini to her, then turn and make for the changing rooms on the other side of the pool, already fighting a growing interest in my trousers.

Christ. How am I going to be able to manage this?

In the changing room, I pull off my clothes and try on the Speedos. Yep. Tiny. They're bright red too and suggestive of sexy French arthouse films from the 1980s, which, from the few I've seen, heavily feature mental health breakdowns and cunnilingus.

Not inferences I want to be projecting right now.

Wrapping one of the large bath sheets loosely around my

waist, I walk back out to the pool. Luckily, Dee hasn't emerged from her changing room yet, so I hurriedly pull off the towel, drop it onto one of the loungers and dive straight into the deep end of the pool.

The feeling of the cool water is bliss on my flushed skin and I swim underwater for most of the length of the pool, emerging with a gasp as my head breaks through the surface.

At least that's shocked my body into some sort of obedience.

Until Dee walks out of the changing room in that bikini.

A pulse begins to beat hard in my throat as I watch her walk to the side of the pool. I'm immediately hot all over again and my cock has sprung back to attention.

Bloody hell.

At least she won't be able to see the bulge in my Speedos while I'm in the water.

Giving her a quick nod, I turn and swim off in the opposite direction, choosing a fast front crawl so I don't have to watch as she gets into the pool. The water drags against my erection, making it hard to concentrate on my strokes.

So much for exercise being the cure for sexual desire.

I swim fast, up and down the pool, length after length, trying to blank my mind of sexy things. But the vision of Dee in that bikini is emblazoned on my mind. I try to turn my thoughts to something else, *anything* else, but the only thing that comes to mind is the expression on her face yesterday after she'd made me come. She'd been jubilant. Like she'd won a prize.

I swim harder, my sharp intakes of breath searing my lungs and my muscles burning with the effort of pulling me through the water.

Finally, I begin to get into a rhythm with the exercise and my mind quietens as I let the repetitive movements soothe me.

After fifty lengths, I finally stop and cling onto the side of the pool, catching my breath and enjoying the endorphin rush. Once my panting has quietened, I look around for Dee and see she's lying on one of the loungers in her bikini. Her eyes are closed and she's stretched out as if she's asleep.

The wind is howling loudly outside now and beating the rain against the large window. It looks wild out there. Uncontained. Unruly.

The parallel with my state of mind is not lost on me.

Hoping Dee doesn't choose this moment to open her eyes, I move to the steps and climb out of the pool, making straight for the towel I've left on the lounger a couple away from where she's sitting. If she sees me in these Speedos, I'm never going to hear the end of it.

I'm just wrapping the towel around my middle when I hear a low, tinkling laugh coming from her vicinity.

Dammit. Busted.

'Nice swimmers,' Dee says with a twist of cheeky mockery in her voice. 'You know, if anyone had suggested the highlight of my time here on a private Greek island was going to be seeing you squeezing your – not insubstantial – packet into a pair of the tightest briefs I've ever seen on a man, I would have told them to *shut the front door.*'

'Yeah, fine. Go ahead and laugh. I don't care,' I say, shooting her a nonchalant grin.

I'm just going to have to style this out, or she'll not shut up about it if she thinks I'm embarrassed by her seeing me dressed – or rather undressed – like this.

'It seems to be the theme of this week,' I say, 'catching sight of each other during clothing malfunctions.'

She throws her head back and gives a full-throated laugh at that.

A tingle runs all the way down my spine at the sound of it.

And it suddenly occurs to me what else she said. *Not insubstantial packet.*

My body floods with pleasure at the compliment.

Keeping the towel wrapped firmly round my middle, I sit on the lounger next to her, training my gaze on the stormy tableau in front of us.

But in my peripheral vision, I can't help but see her shift on the seat and rearrange her long limbs.

I stare harder at the trees tossing in the wind.

After only about thirty seconds, Dee shifts about on the lounger again, sighing and fussing about with the head-pillow bit, her toned stomach tensing and flexing.

She's a natural-born distraction.

'You okay?' I ask, hearing an unintended sting of irritation in my voice.

There's a short, loaded pause before she says, 'As okay as I can be, trapped in the company of a sexually repressed pedant, in the middle of a howling gale, with no way out of here for the foreseeable future.'

But there's a definite smile in her voice.

I can't help but grin. 'I love that you say exactly what comes into your head the moment it occurs to you. That sort of confidence is something else.'

'You *love it* like you think it's great? Or you're being your usual sarcastic self and it actually annoys the crap out of you?'

'Actually, both. Depending on how much sleep I've had.' I turn to raise an eyebrow at her in a show of jest, but she just rolls her eyes at me then turns away, colour rising on her cheeks.

Sexually repressed? Hmm. Well, I suppose she has a point there. I definitely feel like I'm repressing my sexual urges right now. No thanks to our current situation.

The bathroom scene once again flashes through my mind and I feel myself get hard for the millionth time today.

Dammit!

'I'm going back to the room for a shower,' I say, rolling off the lounger on the side facing away from her, then quickly diverting into the changing room to grab my clothes, before making straight for the sliding door.

'En-joy,' she says in a lazy, I-really-couldn't-give-a-shit-what-you-do drawl.

My blood is still pulsing hard through my veins as I stumble into our room. Now that her dad and Jeff aren't here, I should probably move into the room Tim was staying in. A bit of space is exactly what the two of us could do with now. I'll move my stuff once I've had a quick shower.

Just as I'm coming out of the bathroom after sluicing off the chlorine, Dee comes sauntering into the room, still wearing her bikini – and nothing else.

'Are you going to hang about in just that all day?' I ask her irritably, dragging my gaze away from her lithe body.

It's clear she knows exactly what effect she's having on me and she's deliberately teasing me about it now. I mean, she's always loved to mess with me, but this now seems to be her favourite way to entertain herself while we're here.

'Why? Does it bother you?' she says, her expression all mock-innocence.

'No.'

'You sure?'

'Yep.'

'Uh, huh.' Her tone suggests she's calling bullshit.

Which, to be fair to her, it is.

'Why do you feel the need to provoke me all the time?' I

demand. My blood's up now and her semi-naked presence here is seriously fucking with my head.

She scowls at me. 'Because you seem to think it's okay to treat me like I'm just some *nuisance*!'

'Only because you are a nuisance,' I say through gritted teeth. 'You're always *bothering* me.'

'So I do *bother* you then?'

'Yes! You bother me! You're driving me crazy!' I shout back.

'And you're driving *me* crazy by leaving me hanging, then kissing me and messing with my head!'

There's a tense silence as we both glare at each other, breathing heavily, the air vibrating between us.

As much as I don't want to, I can't help but think how sexy she looks, with her cheeks flushed and her eyes flashing fire at me.

And she's not wrong. I haven't made any effort to repay her for my orgasm yesterday.

My heart thumps hard against my chest.

I'm suddenly full of energy.

So full, I'm shaking with it.

Ah hell.

I really shouldn't do it – the idea that's crowding out all other thoughts in my mind.

I really shouldn't.

But I really want to even things up between us so I can stop thinking about it. About her.

Striding to where she's standing, I slide my hand into her hair, tilt her head back and bring my mouth down onto hers, hearing her gasp in surprise.

She doesn't push me away, though; instead, she slips her hands around my hips, then down to cup my buttocks, pulling me against her so my erection presses into her bare stomach. She kisses me back hard, parting her lips to allow me to thrust my tongue deep inside her mouth.

She tastes amazing. Like pure need.

It's another rough kiss, just like the last one, where we're both fighting for control of the situation. Both determined to get one over on the other.

One of her hands slides around my thigh towards my cock and I stop her by putting my own hand over hers and moving it away. Then I guide her backwards until she's pressed up against the wall.

'You don't get to call all the shots,' I say firmly.

'Argh! You're such an exasperating bastard!' she grumbles.

'And you're a demanding bitch,' I reply, moving my hands up to cup her breasts, feeling her nipples harden under the press of my thumbs. Then I slide them down her stomach – sensing her quiver under my touch – to the top of her bikini bottoms, where I hang out for a bit, dipping my fingers into the top of the band, but no further.

'You're driving *me* crazy now,' she complains, but her voice is light with lust.

'Yeah? Well, you deserve it,' I say with a smile, then kiss her again, feeling her mouth soften and mould under mine.

'Hate sex it is then,' she says, grinning back at me when we come up for air, her voice a low rumble in her throat.

'To release the *fucking frustration* of having to be around each other,' I mutter.

'Exactly.' Her eyes are wide and pleading now. 'Touch me properly,' she begs. 'Please.'

That invitation is what I've been waiting for, so I slip my hand fully inside her bikini bottoms, moving my fingers lower and lower until I feel the soft heat of her pussy under my fingertips.

She sucks in a deep breath as my fingers explore her, learning this bit of her body. I've never touched anyone like this before and my heart is racing at how intensely exciting it is to be this intimate with someone. With Dee.

I'm acutely aware that I don't have any real-world experience with this kind of thing and the fear of getting it wrong is keeping me just about in check. I have to make sure I stay in control of this.

'Just fooling around, though,' she murmurs against my mouth. 'We shouldn't have full sex.'

I pull back to look her in the eye and still my movements. 'No?'

'No,' she says. 'It's just a bit of fun, so better not to get too serious. Your first time should be with someone you really care about. So we're just playing right now, okay?' she says again, her voice breathy.

'Yeah, sure. Okay,' I say, though I'm actually a little disappointed she doesn't want to go further. But I get what she's saying. It'll be easier to keep emotions out of this if it's just a bit of light-hearted fun.

'Good.' Pushing into my hand, she gives a small groan. 'Just don't stop doing that.'

She then proceeds to tell me exactly where to press my fingers, how hard and how fast – or slowly – until her breathing becomes rapid and rhythmical on my neck and her skin is hot to the touch.

'Yes, just there. Right there... Don't stop,' she moans, her body starting to quiver and buck against me.

There's a moment of utter silence, then she finally lets out a long, low cry of pleasure, the volume and total abandonment of the sound surprising me. It's like a primal scream, something she's not able to control.

Fuck.

I made that happen.

Okay, I see now why people become so obsessed with sex. The power you feel when you give someone that kind of pleasure is something else.

She continues to shudder against me as her orgasm seems to go on and on, until she finally stills and presses her forehead against my shoulder, her breathing starting to slow.

'Jeez, I really needed that,' she mutters.

'Yeah, I could tell. You were pretty vocal about it.'

I feel her body shake again, this time with laughter. 'I'm not usually that loud when I come.'

'Oh. Right.' I'm acutely aware that I'd not know if that was unusual. I have a lot to learn.

Finally, she raises her head and looks at me. 'It was super intense. I guess from all the pent-up sexual frustration.'

'Uh, huh. Okay, well, good.' I shift a little awkwardly on the spot. An uneasy feeling is growing in the pit of my stomach now. Things have rapidly got out of control here and I'm not sure we should let them go any further. Despite how good it feels in the moment. Who knows where it might lead?

'So we're even now then and you can stop provoking me. That's the end of it?' I ask uncertainly.

She flashes me the most incredulous, mischievous smile I've ever seen.

'Sure it is,' she says, adjusting her bikini, then sliding away from where I've had her pressed against the wall.

I watch her limp away into the bathroom and she shuts the door behind her with a flourish, as if she's the star actor in a play, exiting centre stage.

I stumble to the bed and throw myself onto it, rolling onto my back to stare up at the ceiling, my heart still racing.

What is it about Dee that's so irresistible? No matter how

many times I tell myself it's not a good idea to get sexually involved with her, I just don't seem to be able to remember that in the moment.

My body always thinks otherwise.

And no matter what I just said to her, I have a very strong suspicion that this is definitely not the end of these encounters.

Unless I do something to make sure it is.

13

DELILAH

When I come out of the bathroom in a state of befuddled bliss, I find Jem packing up his bag.

I stop short, my euphoria quickly draining away.

'What's going on? Are you leaving me already? Am I just a one-hand stand?' I mock-pout, though I'm really hoping he's going to tell me not to be ridiculous.

He snorts and shakes his head, but he doesn't meet my eye.

So I guess we're back to being awkward around each other again then.

How disappointing.

What's it going to take for him to relax around me?

My competitive nature steps up, determined to find out. It's like a game, figuring Jem out. One I'm going to win.

'I'm worried if we carry on like this, it's going to make things too... messed up,' he says, still not looking at me. 'We should probably call a halt to it now that we're quits. It's already gone further than I meant it to.'

I go to speak, but he cuts me off.

'Even if it's only a bit of "fooling around", it's not a good idea. I can't... It's not...'

Frustration bubbles up from my stomach. 'Spit it out, Jem, for God's sake.'

He gives a heavy sigh. 'Look, Dee, I just don't have room in my head for this right now, okay?'

I swallow hard.

'Okay,' I say, trying to sound like I'm totally fine with that. That it's no big deal. That I don't have the room in my head either and I can just as easily leave it right here too.

He nods, like that's it, decided.

'Good. But I can't sleep on that sofa again tonight; my back won't take it,' he says, turning to stare at the offending article.

But that's not the real reason, I'm sure of it. He needs his space. So he's not tempted to go back on what he just said.

And I have no argument against it. There's no reason for us to share the same room now that the people we were trying to convince we're in a relationship have gone.

'Okay,' I say again, though I have to admit, I'm a bit gutted. All right, really gutted. And feeling rejected, if I'm honest. Which is ridiculous, but there it is. I can't control the way I respond to these sorts of things, especially around Jem, it seems.

'You're welcome to sleep on the other side of my bed, if you like?' I say, but I already know what the answer to that is going to be.

'Thanks, but I don't think that's a good idea.'

'Where are you going to sleep then?'

'In the room your dad was in,' he says.

'Right. Well, I recommend you change the sheets because he'll have napped in that bed yesterday afternoon before dinner and he's the sweatiest man I've ever met,' I say a little meanly. I know it's childish, taking out my frustration on my dad, but he's the one that forced this weird situation – not to mention abandoning us here on our own while he swanned off with the billionaire – so he can bloody well take the non-embodiment rap for it right now.

'Eww. Thanks for that,' Jem says, clearly not keen on the idea of sleeping in my-dad-infested bedding. 'Yeah. I guess I should find some fresh linen.'

I love that he calls it *fresh linen*. He's so classy. And I'm not taking the piss here, I swear. There are things that hit my pleasure buttons and old-fashioned idioms are one of them.

'We could ask Alina where to get some. I'll come with you to find her,' I say, suddenly hit with the awareness that I don't want to be on my own right now. I think it's the threat of the storm that's doing it. It's unsettling me.

And I don't want Jem to think I'm in any way upset about this turn of events. That's a point of pride now.

'You don't need to,' he says, a little more quickly than I'd like.

I bat a hand at him. 'It's fine. I could do with stretching my legs anyway.'

He just shrugs, as if he knows there's no way he's going to be able to dissuade me, so isn't even going to try.

I pull on my jeans and a t-shirt and we wander out to the entrance hall, Jem a step and a half in front of me.

'I wonder where they are?' I muse.

'Probably in the kitchen. That's where they were when I asked for swimming costumes,' he says over his shoulder, already heading towards a door at the back of the hall.

I stumble after him, still a little slowed down by my gammy ankle.

So by the time I've reached the door to the huge catering-sized kitchen, Jem is already coming back out of it, shaking his head.

'No one in there,' he says.

'Maybe they're in their quarters?' I suggest.

'Yeah, maybe. I'll just check that room at the end. I think it's the laundry. I'm sure I saw that written on the door when I passed it earlier. There's probably a linen cupboard in there.'

'Good idea,' I say, following him as he strides off towards it, still struggling to keep up with him.

So, I'm a few steps behind when he swings open the door to the laundry and I see him stop abruptly in his tracks. His entire body seems to go rigid at what he's seeing in there.

'What's wrong?' I say, making it to the door just as Jem says, 'I'm so sorry!' and goes to swing it shut.

But I still manage to catch a glimpse of what's alarmed him.

I gasp in gleeful surprise, my hand going straight to my mouth to smother the sound.

The sight of Alina, sitting on the worksurface above the washing machine, head thrown back and legs spread wide, with the butler's dark head buried between them – clearly giving her a significant amount of pleasure, judging by the sounds she's making – is now branded onto my vision.

I glance at Jem, who looks back at me, his shocked expression so comical, I can't help but let out a snort of laughter.

He motions to shoo me away from the laundry. 'I'll come back later,' he says, his voice gruff and low.

But I've got the giggles now and I'm having a lot of trouble keeping them under wraps. Hugging my arms around my middle, I lean against the wall, my whole body shaking with mirth.

'Shh, Dee! They'll hear you,' Jem hisses.

'So?' I say, my laughter making it hard to get the word out. With a struggle, I manage to get my guffaws under control.

'They're probably having a good laugh about it... themselves... right now,' I point out between bursts of giggles.

'I doubt it,' Jem replies. 'They're probably really embarrassed.'

'Oh, come on.' I flap a hand his way. 'I doubt it. It's just sex, Jem. Everyone does it. Chill out.'

He starts to stride off down the corridor, his gait stiff with tension. 'Not everyone.'

I hurry after him, as fast as my ankle will allow. He's already back in our bedroom by the time I make it in there and has his bag in his hand, ready to vacate.

My earlier hilarity totally fizzles away. He's still intent on leaving me alone in here then.

I suddenly feel a strong, naughty urge to shock him out of his very fixed attitude.

'You know, it's a lot of fun, oral sex,' I tell him. 'You should try it some time. I can highly recommend it.'

He looks down at the ground and shakes his head. 'Jesus. I wouldn't even know where to start. I've got a lot of catching up to do, sex-wise.'

I lean back against the nearest wall and fold my arms, going for nonchalance. 'Well, luckily for you, I *am* sex wise, so feel free to practise on me at any point, if you like. We could have a whis-tle-stop tour of sexual acts. Get you up to speed.'

Colour appears on his cheeks and he glances at me, blinking rapidly. 'I'm not sure that's a great idea.' His body language says something else, though. Especially the bulge in his shorts. He's going to need to find a way to give himself permission to do this with me, that's clear. He's such a goody-goody.

Which is really dinging my bell.

And knowing Jem, he's going to need more persuasion than your average dude.

So I give a dramatic sigh and say, 'Look, the way I see it, it's just a way to pass the time while we're here. It doesn't have to mean anything. We don't ever have to mention it to anyone. And we'll go back to how we were before we came here, once we're home. I swear, I won't get all obsessed and turn into a bunny-boiler; it's not my style. I have more self-respect than that. And I've got a lot going on in my life at the moment, anyway. I'm not looking for anything serious.'

'Oh, yeah, I forgot, you've got your sights set on your rock-star boss,' he says with heavy meaning, flopping down onto the sofa.

This comment brings me up short.

'Hmm? Uh, oh, yes. Well. He is pretty hot,' I admit.

'And rich,' Jem says.

'I guess.'

What I don't say is that I don't think I'm Jonah's type. And I really want to keep that job. It could be a great jumping-off point to other opportunities. And I'm determined to make a success of my life, despite the opinions of my dissenters.

'But there's nothing going on with him at the moment, I swear. I'm actually more interested in persuading him to let me hang some of my art on the walls in the hotel,' I say, trying to deflect more talk about the state of my relationship with my boss. 'Get it under some noses that have a lot of disposable income.'

'Disposable noses,' he says, the corner of his mouth rising in a lopsided grin.

Cute.

I can't help but grin back. He's such a geek. But a gorgeous one. And he's smart. And quite funny on occasion, I suppose. In fact, I'm pretty baffled about why he's still a virgin.

I walk to where he's sitting and perch on the arm of the sofa.

'How come you've never had a sexual relationship with

anyone?' I hazard to ask since he seems to be in a slightly better mood with me now.

Unfortunately, it appears I've misjudged this because he frowns and says, 'None of your business.'

'Come on, Jem. Talk to me. As a friend,' I say, holding out my hands in supplication.

He shoots me a sceptical look.

'Okay, as a friend of my sister's then.' I pause for effect. 'Or is it *because* of her?'

His sigh is heavy. 'Can we not go there again? My private life is just that – private.'

'Okay. Fine. So does it have something to do with you having to be so responsible when you were so young? Having to be a carer for your parents?' I ask, this time infusing my voice with sympathy. I really want to know what makes him tick. It would make being around him so much easier.

But this change in tone doesn't seem to help either.

'Which part of butt out of my business do you not understand?' he says, springing up off the sofa. 'I'm going for another swim. I've got way too much energy to sit around right now.'

'That'll be all the sexual tension,' I point out.

But he doesn't respond, just walks out of the room without a backwards glance.

I sigh and move to sit in the seat he's just vacated, feeling the residual warmth of him flush my skin, my body humming with an overabundance of sexual tension of my own.

I wish he'd stop being so defensive. It's incredibly challenging to be around him when he's like this.

Hot, but challenging.

To my surprise, he comes storming back into the room a few minutes later.

'The bloody door to the pool isn't opening. Nico must have locked it.'

'Who's Nico again?' I ask, to see if I can get him to reference the scene we witnessed in the laundry and make him blush again.

'The guy with the chinos. The one who was... you know...' He waves his hand about, clearly unable to finish that sentence.

Win!

'Go and ask him to open it then,' I say, suppressing my grin at his adorable awkwardness.

'No way. I'm not going back there right now. Who knows what I'll see if I do.'

I let out a laugh. 'God, Jem, don't be such a prude!'

He gives me the raised eyebrow. 'Sod off. I'm not a prude.'

We glare at each other again, but with more playfulness than anger.

Our accelerated breathing is the only sound in the room.

There's that heavy tension between us again.

My heart is racing now and I'm so turned on, my whole body is pulsing with sexual energy.

'For God's sake, just come here and sit down,' I tell him. I feel like there's only one way to get us past this maddening stand-off and I doubt he's going to be the one to suggest it. Not after what he said earlier.

'I don't want to sit. I'm too jittery.'

'Just bloody sit down, will you!' I snap, pointing at the sofa.

There's a tense moment where he frowns at me, his eyes dark with an emotion I can't read. Then he starts to pace for a few moments, as if he's thinking about walking out again, but can't quite bring himself to.

'Jesus. Okay. Fine!' he says crossly.

Then, to my amazement, he sits down.

'Good,' I say. 'Lean back. Relax.'

He raises one brow. 'Why? What are you going to do?'

'Just chill. You'll like it, I promise. If you want me to stop at any point, just say so.'

'Stop what, Dee?' There's a shake in his voice now. It sounds like excitement rather than fear, though.

I get off the sofa and kneel on the floor in front of him, putting my hands onto his knees. He watches me warily for a second but when he doesn't say anything more, I slowly run my fingertips up his thighs, feeling his muscles tense beneath my hands.

I hear his breath catch in his throat, but still, he doesn't say anything.

When I reach the top of his thighs, I pause for a second, looking into his face, checking he's really okay for me to go ahead with this.

He stares back at me, his eyes hooded, as if he's gone into a bit of a trance.

'Okay?' I ask, just to make sure.

He visibly swallows, then says, 'Okay,' in a rough voice.

The sound of it gives me happy shivers.

Convinced he's into this now, I undo the button on his shorts, slide down the zip, then tug on the waistband of them, along with his boxers, until his cock springs free of its confines.

Jem sucks in a sharp breath and rocks his head back against the sofa cushions, his gaze now trained on the ceiling. A muscle jumps in his jaw.

I take this as a positive sign and grip the base of his erection with one hand, then slowly lower my mouth to the head, letting out a gentle breath against it, before using my tongue to explore the shape of him.

He lets out a low, growly moan and his fingers grip the sofa cushions on either side of him. The muscles in his legs are tense beneath my arms, but he still doesn't stop me or make any kind of move at all. He's letting me do what I want.

The very idea of that excites me.

This is all very new for him, so go slow, I remind myself, finding immense satisfaction in the fact I'm the first person to ever do this to him.

I start to move my mouth and tongue over him, feeling him quiver and buck a little as I tentatively increase the pressure and speed of the movements.

His breathing is fast now and he's letting out more and more groans of pleasure as I continue to suck and lick him, enjoying the salty taste of him on my tongue.

I feel heady with the power of giving him this pleasure, which is a new experience for me. I've had a handful of sexual partners, but they've always been more experienced than me, so I've never got to do anything *new* for them.

'Dee,' Jem pants, and I raise my head to look at him. His eyes are wide and his pupils blown. 'I'm really close,' he says on a long breath.

'Good,' I tell him, 'Come whenever you want.'

He just nods at me, then rocks his head back again.

So I get back to work, keeping my movements regular and firm, using my tongue and fingers to add pressure to the underside and head of his cock, enjoying the rhythmic build-up and the way he's responding to my attention to detail, until he finally lets out a raspy, breathless groan from deep within his chest, slaps his hands against the sofa cushions and comes.

I continue to hold him through his orgasm, feeling him twitch and shudder under my touch and loving the way I've practically brought him to his knees. That I've given him so much pleasure and relief.

I swallow, then release my hold on him and move up his body to press my cheek to his stomach, waiting until he starts to relax.

'Oh my God,' I hear him say above me. 'That was incredible.'

'Excellent,' I say with a smile. Elation ripples through me, giving me more happy chills. 'I loved it too.'

'Really?' he asks.

I look up to see him gazing down at me, his brow furrowed.

'Yeah. I really enjoyed seeing you come apart.' I grin at him and to my relief, he grins back.

'It definitely felt like I was coming to pieces there for a second,' he murmurs.

There's a slightly awkward pause where we just look at each other. It's weird, being that intimate with him, then going back to just being hang-out buddies. But I don't think either of us think there's anything real in this. We're just passing the time here together in the most fun of ways.

I flick away a niggle of dissent in my mind.

It would be pointless thinking it could be anything else. He's made it pretty clear he doesn't see me as the sort of person he could have a serious relationship with. And that's okay. There are all kinds of ways to connect with someone, and this thing with Jem will be sex only.

That's fine with me.

Totally fine.

Totally.

14

JEM

So, what the hell do you talk about after someone unexpectedly goes down on you?

Because I'm a little bit lost for words right now, if I'm being totally honest.

Not that I didn't enjoy it.

I really did.

In fact, it pretty much blew my mind.

And there's the crux of the problem.

It was a hell of a lot better than I ever expected.

Trouble is, I'd told myself it would be absolute folly to get sexually involved with Dee, but I went ahead and did it anyway, because in the moment, I found I couldn't not. Again.

I've never done anything this wild before.

She's a terrible influence on me.

No. That's not fair.

I went back into that room for exactly that reason. I wanted her to persuade me to go back on what I'd said, not ten minutes before. But I was too much of a coward to admit that.

Jesus.

What's happening to me?

It's like I've been put under some kind of spell.

But again, that's not fair.

I'm just as culpable for what took place here.

I pull my boxers and shorts back on, then say, 'Come here,' holding out my arms in a gesture of thanks, hoping for a hug.

Because I am grateful to her. She may push my buttons in a way I find difficult, but at least she makes things happen. Things I'd probably never have the guts to initiate myself.

I guess that's exactly why I'd find her so tricky to navigate a relationship with – she doesn't do things by the book.

It's unsettling.

And extremely exciting.

In equal measure.

To my relief, she gets up from where she's been kneeling between my legs, then moves into my embrace, straddling me and snuggling her face into my neck.

It's like having a Dee blanket.

It's lovely.

I wrap my arms around her back and pull her close, enjoying the sensation of her breath as it tickles my neck.

'So, are we doing this then? Everything but full sex?' she asks me, her voice a little muffled against my skin.

'Yeah,' I say, 'it seems we are.'

She moves her head so she can look me in the eye. 'Are you sure? Because I don't want you to feel railroaded into this. It's supposed to be a bit of fun, that's all. So if you're not entirely sure, speak now and forever hold your own cock.'

I feel a grin tugging at the corners of my mouth. I have to give her that: she can make me smile like no one else I've ever met.

'Yeah, okay. I'm in. If you are?' I say, ignoring a jab of

conscience. She's the one setting the terms here, I tell myself, not me.

'All the way, baby,' she says, moving in for a kiss.

And it's the sweetest thing ever. And by sweet, I mean hot and heavy and immediately erotic in ways I've only ever dreamt about.

'Hey. Do you want a drink? I'm parched,' Dee says, pulling away, then swinging her leg off me so she can sit back on the sofa, then carefully get to her feet.

'Sure. I'd love one.'

I watch as she fills us both a glass of water from the bottle on the dresser.

'Thanks,' I say, taking the one she proffers to me.

We both drink in silence for a moment, the sound of the storm outside acting as an unnerving soundtrack to this bizarrely cosy scene.

So, what now? What do we talk about?

This has to be the oddest situation I've ever found myself in. And yes, I know that makes me sound like a total noob, but I've been a bit busy for the last few years.

'You know,' I say when she sits back down next to me on the sofa, 'I've never seen any of your art.' That has to be a safe topic of conversation, doesn't it?

Tilting her head and frowning, she says, 'You've never asked to.'

'Can I see some now?'

She blinks in surprise, then pulls her head back in a comical, *seriously?* kind of move. Then when I just look at her expectantly, she says, 'Really?'

'Yes.'

'Err, okay. Sure. I guess I can show you some on my phone?'

She suddenly looks nervous, her lip quivering.

'You don't have to if you don't want,' I say, unsettled by the flash of uncertainty in her eyes.

'No. It's fine. Let me just grab my phone and I'll find some I'm happy to show you.'

'Are there some you're not happy with?' I ask, intrigued by her flash of anxiety.

'A couple.'

I watch her walk over to the nightstand next to the bed and pluck her phone from it, then saunter back to me – as elegantly as she can with her ankle still paining her.

I suppress a smile.

Flopping back onto the sofa, she starts scrolling through her Photos app, holding it at an angle so I can't see what she's looking at.

'Here you go,' she says, showing me the screen now. 'I think you'll like this one.'

It's a painting of Bea. And it's knockout good. It really captures the essence of her, her expression shining with kindness and warmth.

'Wow, that's seriously fantastic,' I say, staring at it. 'Have you shown this to Bea?'

'Not yet. I might give it to her for her next birthday,' she says, sounding a little shy about it.

'You should. I'm sure she'll love it.'

Her smile is wide and delighted. 'Thanks.'

'I guess it's only natural you're that way inclined – having a professional artist for a mum. Was it her that inspired you to take up painting?' I ask, handing back her phone.

'Err, maybe. To begin with.'

'I can just imagine the two of you, working side by side in a studio, covered in paint. It must be great having someone you can go to for feedback if you need it.'

Dee snorts. 'No chance. I never show my mum my work. Not after I let her see the picture I was submitting for my A level final project and she absolutely tore it apart. Eviscerated it, actually. I don't think there was a single thing she liked about it. She's a bit like that, Mum – very *opinionated* about very specific things: what I wear, who my friends are, how much fun I'm being, or not, and especially how good my art is.' She pauses and seems to consider what she's just said. 'Yep, that's about it. Everything else is of absolutely no concern to her.'

'Bea told me she's a bit self-involved.'

'No kidding. She's not interested in anything that doesn't revolve around or reflect well on her. And the woman doesn't pull her punches.' She draws up her knees to her chest and wraps her arms around her shins. 'I know I shouldn't care what she thinks, and I mostly don't about the rest of it. When it comes to my art though, it cuts deep. I tell myself it's just one person's opinion, but her comments about that particular picture hurt like she'd slashed my soul with a knife. I loved that piece; it felt really personal to me. I even dreamt about it, that's how invested I was in it. Until she pointed out everything that was wrong with it. How naïve and predictable it was. How uninspired. I could barely look at it after that, I was so embarrassed, and I stashed it away and submitted something else at the last minute, something less "juvenile". It got a decent enough mark, but it didn't exactly wow the examiners.'

'Oh, shit, Dee, that's awful.'

She shrugs, like she's over it, but there's something in her expression that tells me it's still raw. That she does care. More than she wants me to know.

Hell, no wonder she can be so defensive. Feeling like she's only worth being around if she's being fun and creative, but not competing with – or, I suspect, outshining – her mum, must weigh heavy. And having something that's come from your heart torn apart by the person who's supposed to love and nurture you has to be tough to get past.

'At least I got her attention,' she says with a lopsided smile.

But she's definitely forcing it.

'Which is no mean feat,' she goes on. 'Especially when she's deep into making her own art. She's never exactly been the engaged, mothering type.'

'No. It doesn't sound like it. But at least she didn't put you off doing what you love.'

She picks at a thread on the sleeve of her t-shirt. 'To be honest, I very nearly gave up painting at that point. But Bea convinced me to carry on. She was really sweet, as well as practical, about it. She said she thought Mum might have been jealous of me, of my talent, but I'm not sure that's really the case. Her style is way different to mine. And she's got a lot more experience than me, so she knows what she's talking about. She's sold a lot of her pieces too. Though often not for the sort of money she thinks they're worth. I think she was probably trying to give me a life lesson or something. About how tough and competitive the art world is and how thick a skin you need in order to have a successful career as an artist.'

'Tough way to learn that lesson. Especially from your own mum.'

'Ha. Yeah, I guess.' She shrugs. 'It is what it is. Lots of people have a much rougher time growing up than I did, I know that. At least there was always food to eat, even if someone other than her usually ended up making it. The benefits of communal living.'

'You didn't mind living like that? It sounds exhausting,' I say.

She shrugs. 'Not really. It was a bit noisy sometimes, I guess. But that never really bothered me like it did Bea. And it was fun a lot of the time. Always new people coming and going. Like having an ever-changing extended family.'

I cock my head. 'Is that why you chose to live with her, rather than with Bea and your dad? If you don't mind me asking?'

This is something that's always baffled me. Their mum sounds like a completely absent parent, so why not stick with the one that's actually invested in your upbringing?

She throws up her hands. 'Ugh! There's no way I could have lived with my dad. You've met him; he's a complete tyrant. All we do is row when we're around each other. And he's never been that interested in me, anyway. I just don't cut it. Bea's his golden girl. I just figured I'd leave them to it and forge my own path. Even if it meant doing it mostly on my own.' She runs a hand over her hair and I realise her fingers are shaking.

'And honestly,' she adds, 'I get the feeling my dad's always lumped me in with his feelings about my mum. I think he feels betrayed because I chose to live with her. But I would have been miserable living with him. Never being able to please him. I had so much more freedom, living with my mum. And even though she wasn't always there for me when I needed her – particularly when I needed some support about my career as an artist – at least she didn't suffocate me. I know, deep down, he probably does love me, but he just can't bring himself to show it. He's punishing me because my mum left him.'

I nod slowly. 'Yes, sure, I get that. But can you also see that he's now trying to buy your love with the promise of paying off your student loan? If you want him to truly respect you, you need to find a way to live without his financial support or he's never going to take you seriously.'

The returning nod she gives me is jerky. 'Yeah, I hear you on that. I was shocked when he offered it and I guess I just agreed to it because it was easier at that point not to make a fuss, so our ruse would go more smoothly. Not that having my loan paid off wouldn't be amazing. But I'd probably feel shitty about it later. I want him to do things like that for me because he thinks I deserve it, not to appease me, or control me in some way.'

She shrugs and gives me a tight smile.

'At least Bea's always genuinely been there for me when I've really needed her. Especially in the last year or so. It's been lovely getting closer to her, now we're both living in the same city again.'

'Yeah, she's really loved that too, so she tells me.'

There's another heavy pause as we both think about Bea and shuffle a little in our seats.

'Anyway, the whole episode with my painting taught me that people are very quick to judge others' work, even – and sometimes especially, in my mum's case – if they've not put out anything themselves, at least not for a while.'

'Yeah. It can be a judgemental old world.'

'True. I guess we're all like that, though. We like to have our voices heard. But as my lovely friend, Sarah, likes to say, opinions are like arseholes; everyone has one. It's just that some honk more than others.' She flashes me a smile. 'I make myself think about that every time I show someone a new painting I've done. I figure, if I like it, then eventually, someone else might too. And you only need to find that one person for it to sell.'

'A good philosophy.'

She shifts on the sofa again, folding her good leg under her. 'Not that many people actually make it to the level of fame where they can support themselves solely by selling their paintings. I'm realistic about that. That's my dad's influence coming to the fore. Which is why I really want to hang on to that job at the hotel and why I begged Bea to help me, just while my leg's messed up. I'm hoping I can keep a roof over my head with the wage I earn there and make my art around it until I get some sort of breakthrough. That's the plan, anyway.'

'Right.'

I realise I'm frowning when she says, 'And yes, okay. I know it was a real imposition on Bea to ask that of her. And you too, I guess. But I swear, the moment she needs something from me, I'll be right there for her.'

'Uh-huh.'

'You seem uncertain about that.' Her eyes flash with irritation.

I hold up both hands. 'No, no. I'm sure you mean every word. And it's none of my business what you and Bea decide between you.'

'But…?'

'No buts. I'm done talking.' I run my finger across my lips in a zipping motion.

I have to admit, I'm impressed by her resolve to carry on, despite the setbacks. She doesn't give up and I'm in awe of her tenacity.

Now I'm giving her a chance to show me the real her, I'm beginning to see past the chirpy, chippy persona to the determined woman underneath, trying to forge her own path despite everyone writing her off before she's had a chance to get there.

It makes me a little ashamed to realise I've been one of those people.

But none of this means I should be seriously considering having a proper relationship with her. I have enough on my plate right now, what with caring for my mum and growing the business. She'd be an energy suck on that – something I don't have the resources for right now.

I'm exhausted as it is.

So I'm just going to treat this as a learning experience. A way to give myself a break from reality for a while.

I figure, when I'm ready to have a relationship, I'll need it to be with someone like Bea. Though maybe not actually Bea. Not now I've fooled around with her sister. But someone who doesn't need any kind of looking after, anyway.

So it's just sex for fun with Dee while we're here. Which will probably only be a day or two, max, surely?

And she seems to be totally fine with that.

I decide to double check.

'So, to confirm – if we keep doing this fooling-around thing, are you really okay to call it quits when we head back to England? Only, I don't have the space in my life right now to date.'

'Damn straight,' she says, her face falling into a semi-serious expression.

'*Sure* sure?'

'Yep. It'll just be a bit of fun, so no straying into *feelings* territory. We'll be tectonic plates, briefly rubbing together.' She gives me a wry wink.

I raise an amused eyebrow back. 'I'm not sure that's the most apt metaphor for our current situation. We're in the middle of a storm here, not an earthquake.' To make my point, I gesture towards the window that's currently being lashed by high winds and rain and is giving off an ominous rattling noise. Despite the strength of the glazing, I'm a little concerned that the whole thing might blow in at any time, which is causing a low-level anxiety to swirl in the pit of my stomach.

At least, I think it's the storm that's causing it.

Dee rolls her eyes at me. 'Earthquakes, *medicanes*, whatever. As long as it's fun and feels good, I'm up for it.'

She flashes me a grin and I can't help but smile back. As I've come to realise, it's impossible *not* to have fun when Dee's around.

Untucking her leg from under her, she shifts on the sofa and turns her whole body towards me. 'As soon as we get home, we'll go back to being plain old "buddies". And I promise you, no bunnies will be boiled afterwards.' She holds up two fingers with the rest of them folded against her palm, which is facing me.

'What does that mean?' I ask, not recognising the gesture.

'It's a Brownie promise guiding sign.'

'A what?'

'You know.' She frowns at me like I'm being obtuse. 'Brownies. The group you can join when you're in primary school, where you can earn badges for doing things like toasting marshmallows over a fire, or building a bridge of sticks over a stream.'

Laughter bubbles out from my throat. 'Very wholesome.'

'That's me all over.'

I raise a sceptical eyebrow.

'Okay, maybe not,' she says, lowering her hand. 'I suppose I did nearly get thrown out for telling Brown Owl to bugger off once when she told me off for larking about while she was talking.'

I can't help but laugh at that too, picturing a miniature, defiant Dee, chin tilted up and with a mutinous expression on her face.

My heart does a strange flip.

There's a pause where we both look at each other, smiles playing on our lips.

Gazing into her face, I have a sudden, strange realisation that I've stopped thinking about her as Bea's pale shadow. She's become an entity all of her own now. And there's nothing pale about her.

She's as vibrant as they come.

I jump as there's a loud knock on the door.

Dee frowns. 'Come in,' she calls, before I can.

The door opens to reveal the butler, Nico.

'Sorry to disturb you,' he says, looking between the two of us.

'No problem. What can we do for you?' I say.

I'm aware of Dee starting to shake a little next to me. Is she laughing? Hmm. She's probably remembering her earlier hilarity about finding him and Alina at it in the laundry room.

I have to work hard to suppress my own grin as the image of the two of them flashes into my head again.

He doesn't seem at all put out by our childish reaction to him appearing here, though. The guy's a class act. 'I came to tell you the helicopter won't be coming today. The weather's still too bad. Maybe tomorrow, maybe the next day,' he says before either of us has a chance to ask.

'Oh. Okay. So definitely no chance of it before then?' I ask stupidly.

'No.' He's clearly having to keep from scowling at me. 'And I'm afraid Sir Jeff's plane is grounded in Tanzania. It's had some engine trouble, so won't be returning to Europe for a while.'

'Oh,' we both say at the same time, our voices edged with worry.

'Sir Jeff has asked me to arrange transport back to England for you, which will have to be on the trains and a ferry. The airports are all closed at the moment because of the storm and all flights have been affected so there's no availability in the next week. No boats are sailing yet either because the sea's too rough.'

'I see,' I say, fighting down a feeling of slight panic. None of this sounds good.

'I'll book you into a hotel in Athens, if necessary, before the overland travel. Please leave it with me.'

'Okay,' I say. 'Thanks, Nico. Keep us informed about any changes to the plan, will you?'

'Yes,' he states, then gives us a polite nod. 'Dinner will be served in the dining room at eight o'clock.'

'Thanks, Nico,' Dee says.

He nods once more, then backs away, closing the door quietly behind him.

'Ah hell,' I say, rubbing my hand over my forehead. It's tense from frowning so hard.

Dee's stopped giggling now and looks at me with wide eyes. 'So we're stuck here for a bit longer. Potentially, quite a lot longer, by the sounds of it.'

'Yeah. I'm going to need to make a call,' I say, anxious to make sure my mum's going to be okay with me not turning up for a while. She sounded pretty confused when I spoke to her yesterday, but sometimes she's clearer-headed and can get a bit tearful if I don't see or speak to her for a couple of days.

'I'll call Bea and let her know,' she says, already getting up off the sofa and moving towards the other side of the room to sit on the bed.

I wait till she's speaking on the phone, then call the assisted-living complex where my mum is staying now. I get my mum's carer on the phone first, who assures me everything is okay there and that Mum's had a good day today. She then goes off to find her to speak to me.

I wait, with my pulse elevated, for her to come to the phone.

I hear a rustle and some breathing, then my mum says, 'Hello?'

'Hi, Mum, it's me.'

There's a short pause where I wonder whether she's going to remember who I am.

'It's Jem,' I add, just in case.

Every time she forgets me, I die a little inside. It's the most horrendous feeling, having your own mum not know who you are – a horrible insight into the grief I'm going to feel when she passes away. It feels like I'm losing her piece by piece, memory by memory, like a human jigsaw slipping through cracks in the fabric of the universe. No wonder they call Alzheimer's the long goodbye.

'Where are you?' she says eventually, and I relax a little.

'I'm on a Greek island, remember? I called you yesterday to tell you.'

There's another short pause, then she says, 'Oh, yes. I remember now.'

But I get the feeling she can't remember that conversation and is just pretending so I don't worry.

'Is it sunny over there?' she asks, breaking into my troubled thoughts.

I glance out of the window at the storm raging around us, bending the trees to almost snapping point. 'No, it's not sunny. In fact, we've been caught in the middle of a storm here so I'm not going to be able to get back to England to see you for a few days. I just wanted to let you know and check everything's okay there.'

There's another short pause before she says, 'Yes, everything's okay.'

I can't quite tell from the tone of her voice whether she's upset about me being away for longer or if she's confused about what I just told her.

'You sure?' I ask.

She lets out a huffy, impatient sigh. 'Yes, of course. I'm fine here. You have fun on your holiday.'

And the line goes dead.

My chest lurches, but I take a breath and subdue the feeling of guilt spiralling through me. There's nothing I can do about it right now, so she's going to have to cope without me for a few days.

Dee's just finished her call too and comes limping back over to me on the sofa.

I look up at her and force a smile. 'All okay with Bea?'

'Yep. Absolutely fine. Of course. I think she's actually quite pleased to still be working at the hotel, to be honest.'

There's a slight pinch to her brow now, as if this bothers her.

'Really?' I say. *Huh.* I'd have thought she'd want to get out of there as fast as possible. Unless Dee's hot celebrity boss has something to do with it.

I push that thought away. That has the potential to get messy too, but I can't worry about it now.

I need to focus on what's going on here.

'Is your mum okay?' Dee asks gently. Even though I didn't say who I was calling, she's obviously guessed who I needed to check up on.

'Yeah. She seems to be all right at the minute. She even recognised my voice and knew who I was, so I'm taking that as a positive sign. I had a word with her carer beforehand and she said she seems pretty content. So that's a relief.'

'Great. So now you'll be able to relax a bit.'

'Hmm. Hope so.' I get up off the sofa. 'I'll be back in a minute,' I tell her, heading into the bathroom. Once in there, I splash water on my face and take a few deep breaths, trying to clear my mind of the residual worry. *There's nothing I can do and she's in a safe place,* I tell myself. *Put it out of your mind for now.*

I'm glad I've been able to have a serious conversation with Dee about what's being going on in my life. It's actually helped lift a bit of the strain I've been feeling over the last twenty-four hours.

So that's something.

Perhaps I was a bit hard on her to think she wouldn't understand. In fact, I think I've taken a lot of things for granted about her.

Not that I should let myself get too comfortable in her company. She's still quite the wildcard after all.

A fun one to play with, though.

Taking one last deep breath, I go back out to the bedroom.

Dee looks up at me from where she's now sitting on the sofa. 'So, I guess we might have a few days to fill before we're home again,' she says.

'I guess so.'

I sit down next to her and she turns to face me, propping her elbow on the back cushion and her chin on her hand. Her citrusy scent envelops me and I breathe it deep into my lungs, feeling my body immediately respond.

'Whatever shall we do to pass the time?' she says with a waggle of her eyebrows.

My mood immediately lifts and all other thoughts trickle away.

'I know what I'd *like* to do,' I say, reaching up to slide my hand into her hair and rub my thumb along her jawline.

She visibly shivers, her eyes sparking with interest.

'And what would that be?' she asks, straddling me again and lowering herself carefully onto my lap.

'Have a guess,' I say.

'I don't need to guess. From the feel of this, it's pretty obvious what's on your mind,' she says, rocking her pelvis back and forth against my clothed erection. 'So I guess it's time to begin that whistle-stop tour.'

Then she leans in and kisses me and I give myself over to pure pleasure for the rest of the day and the night that follows.

15

DELILAH

And so begins my campaign of how to get Jem off in as many creative ways as possible, without actually having full, penetrative sex.

Granted, it's a bit odd to agree to do everything *but* – but I figure, if we can keep it to just playing around, it'll make it easier for us to walk away from each other once this escapade is over. Especially because he's a virgin right now. There's something particularly *connecting* to be someone's first and that's the last thing we should allow to happen – not when there isn't a chance in hell of this becoming an actual relationship.

I don't want the emotional load of it hanging around my neck.

So, for the next couple of days, there's a lot of hand, mouth – and on one occasion, feet – work involved. It's a real blast. I don't think I've had so much fun in ages.

He's getting pretty darn good at making me come too, learning exactly what I like, how hard and at what speed. In fact, he's now playing my body like a pro – in his typically Jem-like precise and nerdy-technique-studying way. He seems to be on a mission to make up for lost time. Which I have to admit, I'm very much enjoying being a part of, especially since my whole being seems to be on sexual red-alert at the moment.

We're keeping it fun and light, though. Teasing and taunting each other into frothy, lusty messes before allowing ourselves that hallowed orgasm.

In between times, we explore the rest of the house, finding more luxury bedrooms and huge, tiled bathrooms, a gym, a sauna and a cinema room with an even bigger screen than the one in the living room. We watch movies, swim, work out in the gym – I love to watch Jem work out; those muscles of his are something else – eat the delicious food Alina brings into the dining room for us and try to ignore the howling of the wind and the thumps and bangs as it batters the house and surrounding land.

I feel pretty safe here though, especially having Jem here with me. He has a real calming influence on me, smoothing away any fears I have about our wellbeing and distracting me in the most delicious ways.

We don't see much of Nico and Alina, apart from when they bring out and clear away the meals. I suspect they're doing much the same things we are, taking advantage of being alone together in the house without Jeff here.

Both Jem and I stay well away from the laundry room, just in case.

Another couple of days go by, with still no confirmation of when we'll be able to get out of here. Luckily, I get a text from Bea saying I don't need to worry about going back into the hotel to work this coming week because Jonah isn't going to be around. He's off for a break somewhere, apparently, and is happy for me to 'work from home' while he's away. This is a massive relief and means I can relax while we wait out the aftermath of the storm. Jem's been programming a lot too while we've been here, so he seems happy enough not to have to rush back to England.

He doesn't say it, but I get the impression he's actually having a fun time here with me. He certainly appears to be anyway, judging by how relaxed he seems and how much more he's smiling.

It makes my heart sing.

* * *

A couple of days later, Nico finally comes to tell us the helicopter will be coming to take us back to the mainland later that afternoon.

There's a horrible lurching sensation in my stomach as his words sink in.

Dammit. Just when I was really enjoying myself.

The wind has completely dropped now and the sun has come back out, shining down on a storm-torn landscape, so it's clearly time to go home.

Poor Jeff is going to be gutted about the devastation it's wreaked on his beautiful island.

There are trees down all over the place, from the looks of it, and a couple of the outbuildings have had their roofs torn off. Jeff's prized garden is an absolute wreck, with plants and shrubs flattened and stripped of their leaves and flowers.

Still, I'm sure he has teams of gardeners and builders who will fix it all the moment he snaps his fingers.

'Would you consider going to work for Jeff if the business with Bea doesn't work out?' I ask Jem idly as we're lying about naked in bed, wasting some time before we need to shower, pack our meagre things and go to meet the helicopter – once it finally lands on the island.

'It's a tempting offer,' Jem says, rolling onto his side to look at me. 'Hopefully, I'll never need to call on it, though. I'd rather run my own show, but a lot of start-ups fail, so I need to be realistic. My mum's care is bloody expensive, so I'm going to need to earn enough money to pay for that soon too.'

'He'd want you to move to London,' I point out.

'Yeah. That's another consideration. I'd have to move Mum with me.' He rubs his hand over his brow. 'Anyway, I'm not going to worry about that right now. Honestly, it's been quite a relief not to have to think about real-world things while we've been here. It's almost been a bit of a holiday, weirdly.'

'Yeah, for me too.'

We look at each other for a beat.

'It's going to be a real wrench going back to our sedate, non-billionaire-style lives in Bath after this,' he jokes, rolling onto his back again and staring up at the ceiling.

My stomach gives a funny lurch as I wonder whether he's thinking about Bea right now.

He'll probably forget all about me and what we've experienced together here as soon as he's back home and deep into working with her again.

I'm just Disposable Dee.

To my horror, my eyes fill with tears.

Turning away from him, in case he looks over at me again, I get up off the bed and stumble to the bathroom. 'I'm bagsying first shower,' I call over my shoulder before closing the door behind me and leaning against it with my arms wrapped around my middle.

There's a hollow ache in my stomach now. It's almost like I'm hungry. But not for food. For something much more unattainable.

I take my time in the shower, allowing a couple of tears to roll down my cheeks. They're immediately washed away by the flow of the water.

What the hell's got into me? Why am I suddenly so morose? I really don't want to feel like this right now.

I knew from the start this was never going to be anything serious. I was the one who pushed that narrative – but only because I knew he'd never agree to anything more.

And I'd been fine with that. Or, at least, I'd thought I was.

I can't now expect anything other than what we'd agreed on, though. I'd promised I wouldn't do that.

Have some self-respect, woman.

Cross with myself, I get out of the shower and towel myself down roughly, welcoming the sting of the friction against my sensitive skin.

I need to pull myself together, pronto.

This ends the moment we're back home. Like we agreed. I'm not one to go back on my promises. Despite my faults, I'm not clingy.

Plastering on a wide smile, I open the door and saunter out of the bathroom – as elegantly as I can with one foot black and blue and still a little swollen. 'It's all yours,' I say with a throwaway swipe of my hand. Like I'm not melting inside at the thought of this ending.

He jumps off the bed and goes for a shower too, emerging just as I've finished dressing and I'm drying my hair.

Determinedly, I keep looking at myself in the mirror and not at his naked, fit – now familiar – body as he moves around behind me, pulling on his clothes in his usual deft way. He moves so precisely; it's always a joy to watch.

I'm going to miss it.

Miss him.

There's a loud knock on the door and when we call, 'Come in!' Nico opens it and strides into the room.

I shut off the hairdryer and turn to look at him expectantly.

'The helicopter has just landed,' he tells us. 'If you give me your bags, I'll go and put them in for you.'

'Thanks, man, but I'm happy to carry them,' Jem tells him, walking over to the guy and proffering his hand.

Nico holds out his own and they shake.

'We really appreciate you looking after us,' Jem says.

'Our pleasure. I hope we see the two of you again,' Nico replies.

My stomach does a slow roll as I realise that's never going to happen. Not the two of us together here again at the same time, anyway.

The same thing seems to occur to Jem, because he just nods and gives Nico a business-like smile.

'I'll leave you to finish packing, then see you out at the helipad. Here are the details for the hotel we're putting you up in until your train leaves tomorrow, plus the information for the rest of the journey,' Nico says, handing Jem a piece of folded paper, before leaving the room.

Jem takes a quick look at it, then slides it into his back pocket.

'Let me guess, it's a five-star hotel,' I say with a grin.

But Jem doesn't grin back. 'Yeah, I expect so. One last step, before we're back in the real world.'

His tonal switch to sensible, straight Jem brings me up short.

I clear my throat, which is tight. 'Yeah, I guess we're nearing the end of this fairy-tale.'

He snorts, but doesn't say anything to that. Instead, he grabs his bag, then goes to pick up mine too.

'It's okay, I can carry my own bag,' I snap, rushing to take it before he can. I don't want him thinking I'm too much of a princess to do something so menial.

It suddenly seems really important to disabuse him of that notion.

'Okay,' he says, holding up his free hand in surrender, as if I've accused him of taking a liberty. 'Just trying to be helpful.'

There's a short, tense pause in conversation while we check we haven't left anything of ours in the room.

My chest is tight with sadness at having to leave our beautiful sanctuary. It's only been a handful of days, but somehow, it feels a lot longer.

A whole other lifetime.

'Let's go then,' I say when it seems we have everything.

I follow him out of the room, giving it one last longing glance, before pulling the door shut behind us.

* * *

The journey in the helicopter is smooth and this time, Jem doesn't try to hold my hand. I don't ask him to either. It's comforting to have him next to me, though. I hate that I get so nervous flying – I don't want him to think I'm being pathetic – but there's no real hint of that in his demeanour. Or perhaps he doesn't care how I'm feeling, now we're on our way out of here.

I try very hard not to care either.

The hotel is indeed five-star, situated in the centre of Athens. It has a feeling of old-world glamour to it, with wooden panelling, heavy brocade curtains and antique furniture in abundance.

We've been put in a luxury suite, which is nice.

More than nice. It's actually breathtakingly swanky.

Jem and I shoot each other looks as we're shown around it by a helpful porter.

As soon as he's gone, we stare first around the room, then at each other.

'Holy shit, this place is amazing,' Jem murmurs.

'Yeah. Old school, but pretty cool,' I say, trying to imbue my voice with nonchalance. I don't manage it though and Jem smirks at my poor effort.

We put our bags down on a handy chaise longue by the window and have a quick explore of the place before reconvening next to the bed.

'So, err, now what?' Jem asks, raising his eyebrow at me. It's so funny how that gesture has turned into something I find appealing now, after hating it for so long. But then, maybe it's because it's lost its condescension, now we're on better terms.

Now we're friends.

If that's even what we are.

It's a little confusing.

We're certainly no longer just nemeses. He's now my nemesis with benefits. Quite the tongue-twister.

And I'm determined to get some more of those benefits before we call it quits.

But I need to keep it light. I don't want him to know how wobbly I'm feeling about this ending.

So I say, 'Perhaps we should test this bed out. To make sure it's going to be comfortable enough to sleep on tonight.' I give him a mock-innocent look, then sit and bounce up and down on it.

I wait, holding my breath, with my heart thumping in my chest, to see whether he's going to turn me down, now we're no longer on the island.

Relief floods through me when something that looks a lot like mischief flashes across his face.

'I like your thinking,' he says with a grin, already pulling his t-shirt up over his head.

He tosses it, without a care for tidiness, onto the floor.

Joy rises from my stomach to my throat, then rushes through my entire body, making my skin prickle and all the hairs stand up on my arms.

Thank the gods and all that's good.

'Hold up. What happened to Jem the Immaculate?' I tease him, looking pointedly at the crumpled garment, then back at his honed chest.

Oh, my lord. How I'm going to miss ogling his hot bod.

But I don't have time to reflect on the sadness that wriggles into my mind because he launches himself onto the bed next to me, then opens his arms, giving me a 'come hither' beckon with his fingers.

I snort in pretend disdain, but the next second I'm in his arms, pressing my body against his and relishing the feel of his hard muscles under me.

He kisses me briefly, then rolls me over onto my back and methodically removes every piece of clothing from my body.

Kneeling up between my legs, he takes a moment to gaze down at me.

He doesn't say anything and neither do I, but this suddenly feels like a significant moment. Like he's committing my naked form to memory.

I let him.

I want him to remember me and the time we've spent together fondly.

Because I know I will.

Another wave of sadness rolls over me and I close my eyes for a second to fight back the feeling.

He takes this opportunity to lean into me and kiss my mouth, his lips soft, but the pressure firm.

I keep my eyes closed as he moves to kiss my face, then along my jaw and down my neck, his breath warming my skin.

My entire body gives a shiver of delight.

I force myself to focus on that. Just that.

His exploration with his mouth continues downwards and I suck in a happy breath as he draws first one nipple into the heat of his mouth, then moves across to do the same to the other, rolling the areola around with his tongue.

Then he goes lower. And lower still, till he's right where I want him to be.

Opening my eyes, I watch in fascination as his head moves between my legs, giving me the kind of attention I crave whenever I'm around him now.

How did it come to this? Only a week ago, we would barely acknowledge each other, save for the odd taunting comment.

And now look.

Or *feel*, more like.

Ooooohhh. He got really good at this. I envy the woman he ends up with.

No. Nope. Not going to think about that right now.

I'm distracted as his fingers move inside me, finding the exact spot I love to have pressed, and I rock my pelvis upwards, which increases the pressure and the pleasure.

I'm so lost to this now.

So utterly, utterly lost.

He continues to drive me wild with his fingers, catching exactly the right spot, over and over again, not deviating from the rhythm or pressure, just how I like it, and I start to let out little cries of frustration. I'm close, so damn close.

But I can't quite get there this time.

I realise with a thump of alarm that it's because I want more. I want everything. To feel him pressing his body into me and his cock moving inside me. For us to be fully connecting in the most intimate way possible.

But I can't ask him to do that. We agreed not to. And I'm terrified it would tip me over the treacherous edge my emotions have been teetering on for the last few hours.

So I'm going to have to make do with the fantasy of it instead. I force myself to turn my thoughts to a made-up scene in my head, one that's been pushing at the edges for a while now. My body responds immediately, the intensity of the sensations he's drawing from me building to a peak again. And finally, finally, I can feel it coming. I'm on the edge of something amazing. Almost there. Almost...

Then he sucks down on my clit and the pleasure peaks, coursing through me in pulse after exquisite pulse. I let out a long, low cry, almost like a sob, my fingers gripping the bedsheets hard.

My orgasm goes on for a long, long time and I ride the waves of it, my eyes tightly shut against the real world.

Jem lets me, not moving away until it's clear I'm coming down from my sexual high.

'Jesus, Jem. I'm going to miss that,' I say on a long out-breath. Luckily, I say 'that' rather than 'you', even in my befuddled state.

Lifting his head, he grins at me.

'I'm glad to know I've got my technique down.'

I force myself to smile back, not wanting to give him any hint that I'm struggling to keep a bewildering rush of emotions in check right now. 'You really have.'

He shuffles up the bed to stretch out next to me and we lie in silence for a moment, the quiet of the room buzzing around us.

'You were right, by the way, about the reasons I've never had a sexual relationship before now,' he says, surprising me out of my jitters.

I turn to look at him, but he's still staring up at the ceiling. 'Because of being a carer for your parents, you mean?' I ask, grateful for the distraction from my internal wrangling.

He nods. 'Yeah. I couldn't just go out and leave them in the evenings, like most teenagers. It wasn't safe for them to be on their own for hours and hours at a time. My mum would get confused and forget to do things like turn off the gas under a pan of Bolognese sauce and nearly burn the kitchen to the ground. It scared the shit out of me the first time it happened. It wasn't much better the second or third time either. My mum was adamant she was just being a bit forgetful though and used to beg me not to tell anyone about what had happened. My dad wasn't well enough to get up out of bed to keep a proper eye on her a lot of the time, so it was down to me to make sure dangerous situations didn't develop.'

'So – what? You never even got to go out to the pub?'

'Not often. And if I did, I didn't drink so I could drive home after an hour or so. Everyone else would go out clubbing afterwards and hook up, but I couldn't do that. I had to stay focused on my folks. There isn't any other family to help out, so it was all down to me. Which wasn't exactly conducive to starting a relationship.'

'No. I can see that.'

'And I was really quiet and pretty shy at school. I never really felt like I fit in there. I had friends, but only male friends. I kept my head down mostly, so girls never seemed to notice me. I spent a lot of my time either learning to programme in the library or gaming at lunchtimes. I ended up in a withdrawn rut which I didn't know how to get out of. Everyone else's lives seemed so distant from mine, so I didn't know how to connect, you know? I just felt a bit... othered. A bit out of step.'

'And when you went to uni?'

'Well, after a lot of wrangling with the health services, I finally managed to get my mum into a place where she'd be well looked after. She wasn't happy about it, but she understood I needed to know she'd be safe without me there so I could be confident enough to go off to study in another city, albeit one I could travel back from within an hour. So she agreed. As long as I promised to visit her lots. Which I did. But with her moving there, it left my dad on his own at home. He wasn't well enough to look after himself properly, even with home help going in every day, so I used to go back every weekend to take care of him and anything that needed doing in the house. At least for the first half of my first year. Until he' – he pauses and swallows – 'died.'

My heart gives a throb of pain for him and I find myself on the edge of tears again. 'Oh, Jem, I'm so sorry. It sounds like you've been through absolute hell.'

'They weren't the best few years of my life, no.'

'But at least you met Bea,' I say through a lump in my throat.

'Yeah. That was a real turning point. She's been a really good friend.'

There's a slightly awkward pause where unsaid words float in the air between us.

I don't think I've ever felt more envious of my sister. It must feel incredible to be so well respected by your friends and colleagues.

I know I'm a lot of fun to be around, but I'm intensely aware that I'm not the sort of person others would come to for help and support. I'm not a serious person. Not a grown-up. At least not in my dad's eyes, and probably not in Jem's either.

All he's seen recently is me leaning heavily on Bea for help, which I guess must make me seem pretty immature.

And I just keep getting things wrong.

Time to change that now, I think. To pull focus.

I want everyone to see me getting on well with my life and be proud of me.

That's all I've ever wanted, to be honest.

As soon as I get home, I'm going to start making plans that don't involve other people getting me where I need to go.

But for now, I'm going to enjoy these last couple of days with Jem. Having fun, not feelings.

'Hey. Can I sketch you?' I ask, reaching for the notepad and pencil on the nightstand that the hotel has supplied.

He sits up. 'Er, yeah, I guess. If you like.'

'Great.' I go to grab a bathrobe from the bathroom and when I come back, Jem is sitting up against the pillows. He's put his clothes back on.

'Hey. Why did you get dressed?' I ask mock-crossly.

'Oh. I thought you'd want me to.'

'Nope. Strip, please. But just the t-shirt if you like. I don't want you thinking I'm a perv.'

He snorts. 'It's a bit late for that.'

I suppress a grin. I'd like to be professional about this and do a good job here because I really want him to think I'm talented. Not that his opinion should matter. Art is subjective, after all, as previously discussed. But to get any kind of praise from Jem is... I don't know, kinda special. Hard won, I suppose. At least, that's how it feels.

I watch with satisfaction as his t-shirt is removed again.

'So how do you want me to sit?' he asks, suddenly looking a bit uncomfortable.

'However you like.'

He shuffles around a bit, rearranges the pillows behind him, then reclines back against them, finally giving me a nod, as if he's happy.

'Comfy?' I ask.

'Hmm. As I'm going to get. This is a bit weird.' He screws up his nose. 'I've never had anyone draw me before.'

'Another first I get to be in on,' I say, trying not to think again about the major one I'd love to experience with him.

I clear my throat of the tightness that's forming there and get to work, focusing all my attention on the lines I'm sketching onto the paper, occasionally glancing up at him to check his form. After spending all this time with him, I actually have it pretty firmly fixed in my head now and could probably draw him from memory if I needed to.

I'm glad I get to do this with him here in front of me, though.

It'll be lovely to have a record of this time we've spent together. So I can look at it later and remind myself I didn't dream it all.

He sits there patiently as I work, except every now and again, he wriggles his nose or stretches his jaw, as if being this still is hard work for him and perhaps a little tedious.

Maybe a bit of chat would help?

'So, if you've been pretty self-sufficient for a while now, does that mean you can cook?' I ask him.

'Yeah, I can cook. I'm pretty good, actually.'

'And you can clean.'

'Yes, Dee. I know how to clean.'

I grin at him. 'And fix things.'

'Yup. I'm pretty handy.'

'Oh, my God. That's really hot. I think you might be my dream man.'

'Maybe you should learn to do all those things for yourself and be your own dream person.'

'I can do all those things. I had to learn when I was living in the commune with my mum. Self-sufficiency was king there, I'll have you know.' I look up at him and catch the amusement on his face. I hold up a reluctant hand. 'Okay, I admit I've never been an amazing cook, but I'm getting better the more I practise, which I'm doing quite a bit now I'm living on my own in my flat.'

'Huh.'

'You seem surprised that I'm domesticated, Jem,' I say in a mock-arch tone.

'No. I—'

'You know, I think you think of me as some kind of wild animal,' I tease, enjoying the ashamed expression on his face.

'I didn't mean to suggest that.'

'Sure you didn't.'

'Seriously. I'm sorry if I gave that impression. It wasn't cool of me.'

'Well, luckily you're cool in all the other ways, otherwise I'd have to *never speak to you ever again*.'

The corner of his mouth lifts at that.

'No smiling! You'll ruin the picture,' I say. 'This is supposed to be a serious work of art I'm creating here.'

'Yes, maestro,' he says, still fighting his smile.

My heart flips.

Making Jem laugh has to be one of the best achievements of my life.

We're quiet for a few minutes while I start to shade in the picture.

'Don't take this the wrong way,' Jem says, making me jump a little.

I tut as the pencil skids outside the line of the drawing.

'Take what the wrong way?' I ask warily.

'If you really want to be a professional artist, you're going to have to properly commit to it. I don't want to be harsh, but just hanging your paintings in the hotel probably isn't going to cut it, unless you get really lucky.'

I nod, but don't say anything.

'At the risk of sounding dickish like your dad,' he goes on, 'you need to put yourself out there and make it happen. Work your arse off. Network and push and push and push. Get knocked down, then get back up again. Grow a really thick skin. Sorry to be brutal about it, but you can't just sit back and wait for success to happen to you. Unless you're willing to put yourself out there – put yourself on the line – it's not likely to happen. You'll get comfy and end up working at the hotel indefinitely. Which is great, if you think you'd be happy doing that. But if not...'

His words sink in hard. He's not wrong. I know that.

I nod. 'Like you and Bea are doing? Throwing everything at it?'

'Yeah, I guess so. It's a risk. The business might fail. It's statistically likely to. But I figured, if I don't do it now and just get a job working for someone else, I might get sucked into it and tied down, financially and practically, so I may as well shoot for it while I have the opportunity. At least, that's what I've been telling myself. It has to work out soon though or I'm not going to be able to afford Mum's care needs once her savings run out.'

I swallow and nod, not able to look at him in case he sees the tears that are rimming my eyes.

He's such a cool guy. I desperately want things to work out for him. He so deserves them to.

'Well, with you and Bea being so focused and determined to make it happen, you're bound to be successful,' I say, forcing a jollity into my voice I don't feel.

There's that sensation of envy bubbling up from my stomach again that I don't want to acknowledge. It's dark and mean and I absolutely don't want to give in to it.

No. *No*. I'm not going to let it ruin my last night alone with him.

With a huge effort of will, I push the feeling down hard and keep working on the sketch for a few more minutes until I'm satisfied it's as good as it's going to get. I'm actually pretty pleased with how it's turned out. It's captured the essence of him, I think. His astuteness and his kindness too. It's all there in the expression on his face.

'Can I see it?' Jem asks, clocking that I've stopped moving the pencil now.

My heart gives a little stutter. 'Sure,' I say, fighting down my nerves. It doesn't matter if he doesn't love it. Plenty of people don't love a picture that's been drawn of them for all sorts of reasons.

But from the expression on Jem's face when I hand the pad over to him, he does love it.

'Wow, Dee. This is amazing. It looks just like me.'

When he looks up at me, I have the widest smile on my face.

I'm elated by his praise.

He smiles back, his eyes twinkling. His pleasure shining through them.

Oh, my goodness. My whole body feels shivery with delight.

I see now why Bea thinks of him as such a good guy. When you find your way into his circle of care and attention, he's the biggest sweetheart ever.

Not that I'm expecting that to be his MO with me from now on.

I'm guessing that as soon as we're back in Bath and there are other people around – namely Bea – for him to talk to, I'll slide right back down the scale of his favourite people to hang out with. Which is crappy because I'm going to miss his company.

So much.

The thought of never been able to kiss him, or be close to him again, makes my chest ache and I'm aware of a burning pressure behind my eyes and in my throat again.

Even though I Brownie promised I wouldn't get upset about us calling a halt to this fling, I'm not sure how I'm going to be able to keep it.

Maybe if Jem sees me getting my shit together, he'll be more interested in being friends. Or more.

Maybe.

But I'm not going to worry about all that right now. I have more fun things to concern myself with.

Reaching to take the notepad out of his hand, I drop it onto the nightstand, then say, 'Right. Now I've done that, you can take the rest of your kit off.'

He looks amused. 'And do what?'

'You'll see.'

I smile as I watch him strip quickly, his muscles bunching in such a beautiful way under his skin, it sends a rush of desire straight between my thighs.

Crawling over to him, I take the base of his already hard cock in my hand and slowly lower my mouth to it, letting my hot breath fan over him before giving the head a firm lick. I smile as I hear him draw in a shuddery breath of satisfaction.

I intend to play with him for a while and make him wait for his orgasm, though. I love nothing more than to tease him, after all.

And I love being naughty with him.

Brown Owl would be horrified.

16

JEM

After what turns out to be a long, wild night with Dee in the hotel room – where we wind each other up into a sexual frenzy, seeing how long we can edge each other before we're begging to come and finally falling into an exhausted sleep in each other's arms in the early hours – I wake up in the morning still wrapped around her sleeping form, spooning her from behind.

It's the first time we've slept like this. Normally, we give each other plenty of space when we've fallen asleep in the same bed before.

It's both comforting and concerning.

I like the feeling of being close to her like this. Of being protective of her. But I'm also afraid of it. This is not what we agreed. It's getting too serious. Too dangerously cosy.

Not that I should be surprised.

I knew from the moment I met Dee that she'd be trouble. I just didn't know what kind.

I know now, though. Intimately.

And it's not the bad kind really, just... tricky. Like the woman herself.

I have to admit, it's been a little frustrating, keeping to our *no full sex* agreement, but I get why she suggested it. It would bring a whole other level of intimacy and emotional connection to our relationship, which neither of us are looking for right now.

Not that we're actually *in* a relationship.

We're just 'fooling around' as Dee puts it.

I've made sure to make full use of the time we've spent together though, by learning as much as I can about what makes women's bodies tick – or writhe about in ecstasy, in Dee's case.

I've loved every moment of it and I'm really grateful for the opportunity to make up for lost time, in terms of my sexual education.

Dee's been an amazing teacher. Open and vocal about what she does and doesn't like, which has been immensely useful.

I can't quite believe I'm thinking about this in such practical terms, especially when she feels so good, naked and warm and pressed up against my body like this.

There's a sinking feeling in my stomach at the thought of never waking up with her like this again.

Oh, man. It's going to be hella difficult to step away from this thing we've had going when we're finally back at home.

But that's what we've agreed, so that's what we'll do. I can't allow myself to get distracted right now, anyway; I promised Bea I wouldn't.

Huh. Bea.

I guess this thing happening with Dee means that Bea and I can only ever be purely business partners now, at least for the foreseeable future. But, strangely, I realise that's okay with me. It's probably for the best, if I'm being honest. Tim's right; it would be foolish to mix up our business and personal relationships.

She's a good friend and I really don't want to jeopardise that.

I never thought for a second I'd be thinking this because of Dee.

It's funny how life moves in the freakiest of ways, as I've discovered in the last few years.

Who ever knows what's round the corner?

But it can't be a relationship with Dee.

She needs someone wealthy and unencumbered, that'll look after her in the way she craves. Allow her to be a full-time artist. That's not me. Not right now, anyway. And who knows if I ever will be?

And I need to be with someone I don't have to worry about all the time. I have enough concerns as it is with my mum's deteriorating health needs and a precariously developing business.

I need someone safe. Someone who takes life and all its challenges seriously.

Dee stirs against me and for a moment, I wonder whether I should suggest we have one last play before we leave. I decide against it. It's better to call it quits now, before I get any more ensnared in this craziness.

So, reluctantly extracting myself from Dee's warm, soft body, I roll away from her and get up, shaking off a weird sense of unease, and head straight to the marble-walled bathroom for a shower.

When I come out, Dee is awake and sitting up in bed. She gives me one of her mischievous smiles and I nearly change my mind and get straight back into bed with her.

But I resist.

Though it physically pains me to do it.

'Morning,' I say, going over to my bag and extracting the clothes I intend to wear today. Nico kindly laundered all our things when we were on the island, so we've not been in the awkward position of running out of them.

'Morning,' Dee purrs, and my body immediately reacts to the come-hither tone in her voice.

Shit. She's not making this easy for me.

'We should go and grab some breakfast downstairs before heading to the train station,' I say, forcing myself to ignore her implied request to join her.

Her face falls. 'Oh, okay. Yeah, I guess you're right. We don't want to miss the train.'

I turn my back as she gets out of bed and stumbles to the bathroom for her own shower.

By the time she comes out, I'm dressed and have packed up my meagre belongings and I'm trying to force myself to concentrate on some programming on my laptop while I wait for her to be ready to go.

I can feel her looking at me as she moves about the room, dressing and packing, but I don't turn to look at her, determinedly keeping my eyes on the screen.

I feel shitty about appearing indifferent towards her this morning, especially after what we got up to last night, but I feel like it's better to set the tone for cooling things off between us now so it's not so jarring once we get home.

'Okay, Numbers, I'm ready if you are,' Dee says from the other side of the room.

The old nickname brings me up short. It seems like she's understood my implicit suggestion we take some steps back now and is attempting to return to her original form with me.

I suddenly feel inexplicably sad.

Ignoring the discomfort in my chest, I shut my laptop and pack it away into my bag.

'Okay,' I say, getting up from the desk I've been sitting at. 'Let's go.'

* * *

We make it onto the train with plenty of time in hand.

Dee's being unusually quiet, but I stop myself from asking if she's okay. I can't get into it right now. I don't even know what I'd say if she told me she wasn't.

She's not my responsibility.

We find two seats next to each other and stow our bags on the baggage shelf, then settle into our seats. This leg of the journey to the ferry port in Patras is going to take about four hours, so we both sit and stare out of the window for a while at the passing scenery. There's been a lot of storm damage here too and there's a big clear-up job going on. We see flashes of wrecked buildings, felled trees and torn-down walls and fences as the train rushes along the track.

After a while, I get my laptop out of my bag and go back to programming, for something to do. And a way to stop my mind from whirring. I don't feel like chatting today and it seems Dee is the same. She spends her time either reading on her phone or staring out of the window.

Perhaps she's feeling the same poignant weight of this ending, just like I am.

It's hard to tell with her. She doesn't always give a lot away and puts on a happy-go-lucky front a lot. I guess she's well practiced at it, after having to do it from a young age.

When we finally get to Patras, we go straight to the ferry port, as per Nico's instructions, where we get onto the ferry and are shown to our sleeper cabin. There are two single beds in there, which Nico has apologised for, saying the luxury cabins with double beds were fully booked, but I'm actually grateful we won't have to share a bed again tonight. The urge to touch Dee is strong, but I'm fighting it right now, not trusting myself not to get carried away and let things segue back to how they were last night.

Memories of how much fun we'd had flash through my head and I have to readjust the front of my trousers so Dee doesn't see how turned on I am.

Dammit! Stepping back from this thing we've had going is really fucking hard.

But necessary.

We can't carry it on. It would be lunacy at this juncture.

'Which bed do you want?' she asks me, waving her finger between them.

I shrug, still trying to get my frustration under control. 'Don't mind. You choose.'

'Okay,' she says on a sigh. She sounds frustrated too, like she thinks I'm being deliberately unhelpful. Which I guess I am, to be fair.

She sinks down onto the one on the right and flops onto her back while I turn to stash my bag on the luggage shelf. Just at this moment, the ferry lurches as it pulls away from the port and I take a stumbling step backwards, lose my balance and fall back onto Dee's bed, luckily not actually landing on her.

She sits up in alarm and puts a hand onto my arm. 'Whoa there. Are you okay?'

'Fine,' I mutter. The heat of her touch burns through my shirt and tendrils of sensation ripple across my skin. I turn to look at her and she stares back at me.

There's a pulse of silence where we just look at each other.

My heart gives an extra-hard thump against my chest and my breath seems to get caught in my throat.

'Let's not stop yet,' she says quietly.

There's such an expression of longing in her eyes, I instantly forget my resolve and, acting on pure instinct, move in to kiss her on the mouth, the memories of last night – and all the other amazing nights with her – rushing to the front of my mind and reawakening my hard-on.

She responds immediately, kissing me back hard, her hands slipping into my hair and gripping my head. It seems like she's afraid I'll pull away if she lets go, but I'm not going to. Not right now, anyway.

Slipping my tongue into her mouth, I groan as she opens her lips wider and tongues me back. I love the taste of her. She's delicious.

Things move quickly and before I know it, I'm lying on top of her, my knees between her spread thighs and our pelvises pressed together. She's wearing a skirt today so there's not much between us stopping our bodies from being skin to skin. The idea of that thrills me and I start to rock against her, my erection sliding back and forth against her material-covered pussy.

She lets out a low moan of pleasure and grabs my buttocks with her hands, pushing me harder into her.

Oh man, that feels good.

No matter what I told myself this morning, my body didn't seem to get the memo about bringing things to a close.

Her breath is coming fast now, telling me she's just as into this as I am, and she gives another little moan of pleasure as we increase the rhythm of our movements.

We've not dry-humped before and it's hotter than I could have imagined.

But I want more. I need more. I have a sudden, urgent need to finish this on a high.

'We could… you know,' I mutter against her mouth.

'Could what?' she gasps.

'Have sex. Complete my education.'

My words seem to take a moment to sink in, but when they

do, she puts her hands on my jaw and pushes me away so she can look me in the eye. But it's not an expression of excited agreement I see there.

She's frowning.

I slow my rocking, unease taking over from sexual hunger.

'I don't think we should,' she says.

'It'll be fine,' I say lamely, my frustration at having to stop now getting in the way of common sense.

'It won't be fine,' she says, putting her hands against my chest and pushing me away from her.

I roll off her and get up, then go to sit on the side of my bed, opposite her, my breathing still accelerated and my mind buzzing.

'It would be crazy for us to have sex now,' she says, sitting up too and swinging her legs over the edge of the bed so she can face me. 'Just when we're about to stop doing this. It's been fine up till now, just fooling around, but actually having sex would be a step too far.' She rubs her face with her hands. 'We should wrap it up now, not make things even more complicated.'

'It doesn't have to be complicated. It would just be fucking. It doesn't have to mean anything,' I say, though I know I'm talking shit right now.

She knows it too because she says, 'But it should! You should lose your virginity with someone you really care about. Probably with someone you love.' There's a tremble in her voice now and a beseeching look in her eyes.

And that's the moment I realise things are in danger of tipping over here. She wouldn't be acting like this if the thing we've had going was only a fun fling and meant nothing more than that to her.

The realisation brings me up short.

My pulse has picked up and I suddenly feel panicky and out of my depth.

When I continue to just stare at her and not respond to her implied question, her gaze flicks away from mine. I see her swallow and she blinks rapidly, as if fighting back tears.

I clear my throat, feeling tension there. 'Yeah, okay. Of course, you're right. Sorry. I shouldn't have pushed it,' I say, at a loss for what to say to make this better. Which I can't. I've well and truly fucked up.

Getting up from the bed, I run my hand through my hair, then walk to the door and turn to look back to her.

'I'm going to go for a walk on deck to get some air and give us both a bit of space to cool down. I'll see you in a bit, okay?'

Her eyes are wide and still rimmed with tears as she stares back at me.

I hate feeling like this, but it's the sensible thing to do to stop it here. I can't give her what she needs from a real relationship right now, and there's no point in pretending I can.

I don't want to give her the wrong idea about how I feel about her and for her to hate me for it afterwards when it doesn't work out between us.

Turning away, I walk out of the cabin, closing the door quietly, but firmly, behind me.

* * *

I spend a bit of time wandering around the deck, then get a drink and sit on my own for a while, mulling everything over but coming to the same conclusion that I did in the room. This can't go any further between us.

I can't allow her to get into my head right now.

Further in.

She was right to stop things when she did.

When I get back to the cabin, the lights are out and Dee appears to be asleep, her back turned towards me.

I don't wake her up and quietly get ready for sleeping, then get into my own cold, single bed and pull the covers over me.

I don't manage to fall asleep for ages.

* * *

When I wake up the next morning, Dee is already up and dressed and sitting on her bed reading something on her phone.

She looks over at me as I sit up and pull the blanket off myself.

'You've slept late,' she says, in what sounds a bit like an accusatory manner. As if I was up late last night partying without her.

Ah, hell. I've clearly really upset her and she's going to give me the cold shoulder now, I expect.

But to my surprise, she then flashes me a grin and says, 'I grabbed you some breakfast from the buffet. They were starting to run out of the good stuff when I was there earlier and I didn't want you to have to put up with the scrag ends.'

'Oh. Right. Well, thanks, I appreciate it,' I say, giving her a nod. 'Very thoughtful of you.'

She quirks an eyebrow at me. 'I do think about other people sometimes,' she says, but there's no sting of reproach in her voice.

I'm grateful for her maturity about this. I was expecting her to ignore and/or berate me today, so this is a welcome outcome.

I go and get showered and dressed in the titchy en-suite and come back out to find she's put the plate of food she picked up for me on my bed.

'Thanks,' I say, sitting down to eat it. I'm hungry this morning. Ravenous, in fact.

Dee goes back to reading on her phone and I'm glad of the reprieve from having to make awkward conversation. I'm still feeling shitty about how things went last night and aware we've still got some intensive time together before we're back home.

It's not long after I've taken the last mouthful that they announce the ferry is pulling into the harbour at Bari.

We dutifully pack up our scarce possessions in silence and make our way out to the passenger exit, ready to disembark.

I'm antsy now. Not sure how to act or what to say. But Dee seems almost serene. Like she's crossed over to the other side of something I've not been invited to join her in.

It feels... weird.

The transfer between the ferry and the train to Milan goes without a hitch and we're soon in our seats and speeding along the Adriatic coast, taking in the magnificent scenery.

Still, she doesn't ask me any direct questions and only answers my own queries with the sparsest of detail. She's definitely holding herself back now. Giving me the space I asked for.

Huh.

This part of the journey seems to take forever and I get a lot of work done in between the regular leg stretches, snacking and napping we do whenever necessary.

Dee's a good travelling companion, it turns out. She can actually entertain herself – despite my previous mean-spirited suggestion that she needs other people to keep her amused – and is always alert enough to hand over tickets or passports whenever called upon to do so.

Which is helpful for me when I'm in the middle of writing a line of code and can't bear to be interrupted in case I lose my train of thought.

We actually seem to bumble along okay.

I think she's trying to prove something to me.

But I suspect this will only ever be a short-term swerve, now it's become clear there's nowhere else for this relationship – if that's what you can call it – to go.

* * *

The next leg of the journey is a high-speed train from Milan to Paris and once we make it there, we manage to get pretty much straight onto our Eurostar connection. Thankfully, these seats recline, so we're able to sleep as the train speeds us to London.

We step out onto St Pancras train station, blinking and yawning, and stumble over to Kings Cross for the final part of the journey.

The Underground is busy, so we have to squish ourselves into a carriage on a Circle Line train to Paddington station. Dee is forced to press herself up against me and for one mad moment, I almost put my arms around her and hug her close to my body. For one last touch. But at the last second, I manage to resist the temptation.

The way I look at it, I'm doing both of us a favour by holding the line here.

Unfortunately, the train to Bath is delayed, so we end up sitting in a noisy coffee shop for forty minutes waiting for it, slowly sipping increasingly cooling coffees as people bustle past us.

We've managed to maintain a basic level of conversation throughout the journey, mostly about practical things, but just as we're getting up to head to our delayed train that's finally made an appearance, Dee turns to me and says, 'So when we get back, do we just pretend to Bea that everything's normal between us?'

I can tell from the stilted way she says this that it's been on her mind to ask it for a while and she's blurted it out now, unable to hold it back any longer.

'I think that's probably the best way to handle it, yes,' I say slowly. 'As agreed, right?' I add, with emphasis.

She just looks at me for a few seconds, as if she's hoping I'll say something more.

But I don't. There's nothing more to say.

Her answering nod is a little jerky and she opens her mouth as if to say something, but then shuts it again. I see her swallow, then she clears her throat. 'We'd better go,' she says, giving me a tight smile.

Oh man, what's going on in her head now?

No. I don't want to know.

I can't get into this.

So I grab my bag and say, 'Yeah, let's go,' and walk out of there and straight to our train without looking at her again.

I'm aware of her following behind me, lagging a little due to her still being compromised by her damaged ankle, but I don't slow down for her.

Once we've boarded the train and found our reservation, she sits in the seat next to me and puts her headphones straight on, then opens up her book app.

I relax a little, relieved she's not going to restart that conversation, and settle back in my seat, closing my eyes.

It'll be a huge relief to finally get back to Bath and the life I've methodically carved out for myself there.

I hope Bea's been okay holding the fort.

I've deliberately refrained from getting in touch with her much while I've been in Greece, bar the odd short, business-focused text, because I wanted to keep this thing with Dee under wraps. I think in the back of my mind I was afraid Bea might sense there was something a bit off or different about me if we talked. Which was probably an overreaction, but I didn't want to risk making this crazy situation any more complicated.

I'm actually looking forward to seeing her again now and getting back into our regular rhythm of work.

There's a strange, unsettled feeling in my belly though and a tightness in my chest. Probably from being exhausted after all the travel.

Opening my eyes, I slide my laptop out of my bag and prop it on the narrow, fold-down tray on the back of the seat in front of me.

Staring at the code on the screen, I try to force my foggy brain into action.

But it's impossible to concentrate. I'm too strung out and tired.

Too aware of Dee sitting quietly next to me.

So I close the lid and put my computer away again.

Glancing at her, I see she's got her eyes closed now.

A rush of something that feels like nostalgia, or a sort of strange *longing*, swamps me and I have to force it down and turn my thoughts to all the things I need to do once I'm back home instead. The top of the list being to visit my mum.

An hour later, we've arrived at Bath train station and ten minutes after that, a taxi delivers us to Bea's flat and we stumble up to the front door.

And finally, *finally*, we're back.

17

DELILAH

I'm putting my key into the lock of the front door to Bea's flat, trying not to let Jem see how much my hand is shaking from the effort of appearing carefree and cool about this thing ending between us, when it hits me that this might actually be the last chance I'll ever get to be alone with him. After this, Bea's going to be around and within earshot and I won't be able to act the way I have been with him in the last few days.

I'm going to have to pretend I don't feel the way I do.

Oh, man, I'm going to miss it so much – the closeness we've shared over the last few days. I've had such a lot of fun with him.

Why does it have to end?

If it were up to me, I'd give a relationship with him a go. A good go. In fact, I think I'd be very happy to fully commit to him.

I know we agreed sexy fun times only and that we'd go back to just friends when we were back here, but I don't know if I can do that any more.

I want more from him. Much more. And I know I was the one to stop us from having sex, but I had to, in order to protect myself.

I couldn't let it mean nothing. Not when it would have meant so much to me.

Because it really would have.

Things are different now, in so many ways. It feels like a lifetime's worth of experiences has happened since we first left Bath to travel to Greece.

That's the thing about spending time away from your normal location: time bends.

I feel kinda different in myself too. A lot calmer and more focused, or something.

Maybe that's from all the orgasms I've been having in the last week.

But I know that if I don't at least ask the question about whether we can turn this into something real, I'll always wonder whether I should have done.

I'm not a big fan of regrets. I'd rather take the heat and be rejected than feel like I missed an opportunity.

And this feels like a biggie.

So I pause, just before I turn the key in the lock, and turn to look at him, my mouth half-open as I try to decide the best way to do this.

He looks back at me expectantly.

'Is it the wrong key?' he asks, a little confused when I just stand there, frozen.

My heart is thumping so hard, I can feel the vibration of it in my throat.

'No. I just... I wanted to ask you something... before we go in and this whole adventure we've been having comes to an end.'

I see him swallow and he shifts on the spot. 'Okay,' he says, though from the tone of his voice, it's not okay. He doesn't want to be having this conversation.

I push away my worry. It needs to be said, just in case I'm reading this wrong and I've misunderstood things.

'Do you think there's any chance we could carry this on? Or turn it into something more at some point? Because I think... I would really like that.'

Heat's rushed to my face and my entire body feels jumpy with adrenaline. I'm aware there must be a pleading sort of expression on my face, which is frankly a little bit embarrassing, but I'm willing to look foolish here if it means I get to keep him.

He sighs and rubs his hand over his face, then shakes his head before looking me in the eye again.

'Look, Dee, I think you're great, but you're not what I'm looking for in a serious partner,' he says, his voice vibrating with emotion.

My stomach drops in a sickening way, like I've jumped off a ledge and realised I'm way too high up to land safely. 'What do you mean by "serious"?' I ask in a quavering voice.

'I mean not just a fling. A grown-up relationship.'

'How about a childish one?' I say, hoping to lighten the mood. This coolness is horrible after feeling so close to him recently.

'No. I don't need that kind of distraction right now. I told you, I have too much on my plate.'

'I can help you. Support you—' I start to say.

'No,' he interrupts. 'You can't. And I really can't have this conversation right now. I'm too tired for it. I'm sorry.'

'Can you at least think about it?'

'I already have and it's still a no. Like I said, it's not what I want.'

Gently knocking my hand out of the way, he turns the key, pushes open the door and steps inside, heading straight for the kitchen.

Frustration surges through me, making my skin prickle all

over as I follow him into the flat. 'Maybe. Yeah, sure. *Maybe* you think I'm not what you want. But I *am* what you need,' I whisper as we walk into the kitchen, aware that Bea might be at home. I don't want her to hear any of this.

Putting down his bag, he turns to face me and rolls his eyes extravagantly. 'Jesus, Dee. What the hell do you know about what I need?' He's angry now. Clearly, he just wants me to stop arguing with him and leave him be.

But I can't.

I just bloody *can't.*

'A lot,' I say. 'Because I need the same thing. Security. Love. Warmth and kindness. Joy and laughter. All the things I've been chasing my whole life.'

He shakes his head, refusing to look at me now.

But I won't have that. I refuse to let him dismiss me again, like he always has.

'Look, I know we can rub each other the wrong way some-times, but you come alive around me. Don't you want that for yourself? To live an exciting, provoking, *full* existence? Rather than one sat in front of a screen all day and all night on your own?'

He still won't look at me.

'Jem,' I say firmly, reaching out to cup his jaw and gently turn his face until he's looking at me. 'We're good together. You know it.'

He shakes his head firmly, dislodging my grip on him.

'Sorry. I can't commit to a relationship with you.'

'Please,' I beg, tears springing to my eyes. 'Please don't do this. To me or yourself. You're throwing away something really good here.'

'I've got too much going on in my life right now,' he says, frus-tration flooding his voice. 'I have to concentrate on the business and my mum's care needs. We're back to real life now, Dee. I can't play any more.'

The smile he gives me is sad, but also filled with the aloofness that's made me crazy since the first time I met him.

And then Bea walks into the kitchen.

I love my sister to bits, but she's being the queen of bad timing right now.

'Hey, you're back,' she says. She looks happy to see us, but there's a strange sort of wariness in her expression too. Did she just overhear what we were arguing about?

On the verge of tears, I walk over and fling my arms around her, pulling her in close.

I need comfort. I need my sister.

'So, you finally escaped from the storm,' she says, her voice a little muffled against my hair.

'Only just,' I say, hearing the weight of sadness in my voice and wishing I was better at hiding my feelings. Bea's going to suspect something's wrong and that's not fair on Jem. I don't want to make this any harder for him than it already is.

'Is everything okay?' she asks, pulling back to look me in the face.

I make myself smile back at her. 'All good. Just glad to be home safe. The journey back was mostly smooth,' I say. I have to force myself not to glance over at Jem.

'So, are you two still speaking to each other?' Bea jokes, looking between the two of us.

There's a heavy pause, then we both say, 'Yes,' at the same time.

Ugh. It must be so bloody obvious that we're not.

I need to create a diversion.

'How about you?' I ask her. 'How did the festival go?'

'Oh. Great. It went really well,' she says, but without the same enthusiasm I've been hearing from her up till now.

'You don't look very happy about it,' I say, frowning. Something's definitely wrong here, I can sense it.

My fears are confirmed when Bea tries to smile, then fails, and tears pool in her eyes.

'I... er... I've got some bad news, I'm afraid,' she says in a very un-Bea-like wobbly voice.

Panic shoots through me. 'Are you okay? What's going on?'

'I made a real mess of things, Dee. I'm so sorry.'

Bea? Make a mess of things? Surely not. 'What do you mean?' I ask.

'I... I had to tell Jonah I was pretending to be you and... he fired me. Well, you. He fired you.'

I stare at her, flummoxed.

Huh. That was not what I was expecting to hear. Whenever we'd been in contact, she'd made it sound like everything was going smoothly. Had she been lying to me? That isn't like Bea at all.

'Right. Okay. And why did you have to tell him?' I ask gently. There's clearly something more going on here than she's been comfortable to admit.

'Um...' She looks distraught now and my stomach sinks at the sight. 'We, er... We started to get close.'

Oh.

Oh.

'When you say close...?' I say, willing her to tell me everything now, though I can pretty much guess the rest.

'We kissed.' She screws up her eyes for a second, then slowly opens them again, like she's peeking out to see my reaction.

I can't help but grin. My perfect, logical sister has fallen in love with my boss. Well, who knew?

Not that I'm happy that she seems so upset about it.

'And he kissed you back?' I ask.

'Yes.'

'Wow. So you two are a thing now?'

She shakes her head. 'No. We ended up sleeping together, but he's really angry with me for lying to him about who I really am. I think it's over now.'

I suddenly remember that Jem's in the room with us listening to all this when he makes a clearing sound in his throat, then excuses himself.

Ah.

I'm not entirely sure how to respond to this. On the one hand, I feel for him that he's had to find out that the woman he's probably in love with is in love with someone else. On the other, I'm selfishly pleased that the two of them may never have a relationship other than friendship or business partners if Bea's heart belongs to someone else.

To Jonah, of all people.

It's funny, but I can actually see them together. They'd be good for each other.

I've never seen my sister so affected by a man before. So much so, it looks as if she's about to cry.

'Oh, Bea! You poor, poor thing,' I say, wrapping my arms around her again. 'Don't cry. At least, don't cry about me losing my job. I don't care about that. I'll get another one. I was never any good at it anyway and I was fooling myself it would all magically work out and help turn me into some famous artist. What was I thinking! Clearly, Jonah wasn't interested in a relationship with me either. He wouldn't kiss *me* back.'

And now Jem won't either.

Even though there's nothing I'd love more.

I was serious about wanting us to be serious, but it seems I'm not serious enough for him.

'I don't know how it happened,' Bea says now, sounding like she's worried I'm angry with her. 'I never meant it to, I swear.'

But I'm not angry. Not with her. With myself, maybe. I'm like a chaos demon, causing havoc wherever I go.

It needs to stop.

I want it to stop.

'Yeah, well. Sometimes these things creep up on us and take us out at the knees,' I tell her.

Just like my feelings for Jem did.

Bea shoots me a pained smile. 'I never believed in love at first sight before. And then I met Jonah.'

'So, you love him?' I ask, though that's been patently obvious from the moment she started talking about him.

'It sounds crazy, I know. I've only just met him, but there's something about him... I just know, deep in my bones, that he's the man for me. It's an instinct, not something I can explain.'

'That's love for you,' I say. She deserves to be happy too, my kind, considerate sister.

'I can't believe this situation. It's so messed up!' Tears are running down her cheeks now and I'm suddenly desperate to make this right for her.

'Are you sure there's nothing to be done here?' I ask gently.

'Yes. I'm sure. You should have seen the way he looked at me when he left. He doesn't trust me any more. He can't. Not after I lied to him the way I did.'

Shame washes through me. This is all my fault. 'Because I made you,' I point out, wanting her to know how sorry I am to have caused her this pain.

'You didn't make me. I chose to do it. I could have said no.'

'Hmm. I'm not sure about that. I basically emotionally blackmailed you into doing it,' I say, echoing Jem's words to me when we were on the island. He was right; I have been selfish. And thoughtless.

Guilt wells in my gut.

'Well, it doesn't matter any more,' Bea says, clearly trying to pull herself together now. 'It's done and can't be undone. We're both just going to have to move on with our lives in different directions.' She takes a deep, steadying breath. 'Speaking of which, I need to let Jem know something. I'll be back in a moment and we'll talk some more and see if we can work out what we're going to do about getting you a new job.'

I open my mouth to tell her that she doesn't need to concern herself with that – that I need to take responsibility for my own life now and she doesn't need to fix it for me – but before I can get the words out, she leaves the room.

I follow her out into the hall, but she's gone into the office to speak to Jem and I hold back from walking in there. It sounds like they have some serious business issue to discuss.

I swallow hard, hearing the solemn tone of Bea's voice and deducing it's not good news.

Taking a step closer to the partly open door, I hear Jem say, 'Sorry, Bea. It's a great opportunity, but it'll be intensive and won't leave me any time outside of it to work on something new with you.'

Oh no. So it sounds like they didn't get the funding they were hoping for and the business is dead in the water. And Jem's already decided to take Jeff up on his offer of a job.

Which means he's going to leave.

I might never see him again.

There's a horrible, squeezing sort of pain in my chest as I consider this.

No, no, no.

Before I can check myself, I push open the door and step into the room. I need to see his face. To see if there's any way I can stop this from happening.

I give a small cough to clear my throat and Jem glances over at me for a second, then turns straight back to Bea, as if my presence there is of no real consequence.

'It's based in London. I'll be working for the guy your dad introduced me to this week. The one who owns the island we were just staying on,' he tells Bea.

'I see,' she says, not sounding entirely delighted about this either. 'Okay. Well, far be it for me to stand in your way. I want you to be happy and if this is the way to make that happen then you have my every blessing.'

'I'm really sorry, Bea. I wanted to make this business work with you, but it looks like it's not meant to happen.'

My sister nods. She's a smart cookie and knows when she's beaten. 'Yeah. We should cut our losses. And you should definitely take that job, if it's something you want to do.'

Jem stares down at his keyboard and nods. 'I think it is.'

I want to cry. Or go over to him and shake him. Do something, anyway, to snap him out of this decision.

'So, you're going to take it?' I blurt.

'Yeah,' Jem says. That's it, just *yeah*. Like it's no big deal.

Like he can just walk away without a backwards glance and leave me here. As if what happened between us means nothing to him.

Bea must sense my pain because she looks between us with her eyes narrowed and asks, 'What's going on with you two?'

'Nothing,' Jem says, getting up from his chair. 'I'm going to head home. I have things to arrange.' As he passes Bea, he reaches over and squeezes her shoulder. I wait for him to touch me too. Just a small acknowledgement that this is tough on me as well. But he doesn't; he just walks past me as if I'm not there.

I let him go.

All right then. Fine. If that's the way he wants to do this, then okay. He can brush us under the carpet if he wants. Pretend there's nothing there between us. I know there is, though. I *know* it.

I'm on the brink of ugly crying, but I know that bawling about this isn't going to fix it. Complaining about it isn't either. You have to have agency in this world to make good things happen for yourself, right? So that's what I need to do. Stop relying on other people to get me where I want to be and figure out a way to do it myself.

I want Jem to see me as an independent, strong woman. Someone he'd be happy to be with – someone he's proud of and has respect for.

And most of all, I want that for myself too.

Even if we never actually get together, I want to be proud of the choices I've made.

I hope we do get together, though.

Because I really care about him and I truly think we'd be great together.

I just need to find a way to prove it to him.

But that's a problem for another day. First, I need to fix the mess I made for Bea. She needs me right now and there's no way I'm letting her down again.

It's time I grew up and started to take life seriously. I understand that now.

'Okay. I'm going to go and see Jonah and sort this mess out,' I tell her.

She blinks at me in surprise. 'What?'

So I tell her all the things I'd like to say to Jem right now. That

I think he's hurting and he's put up a protective wall around himself, but he's making a big mistake. He's going to lose the best thing that's ever happened to him that way.

Then I tell her what a wonderful sister and person she is and that she should put herself first for once. That she doesn't need to act like my mother any more. That I'm taking responsibility for myself from now on and I'm going to fix this for her.

And I mean it too.

Every damn word.

I have a lot of work to do on myself, I know that. And this is the perfect way to kick-start it.

18

JEM

Three months, three weeks and four days later

The move to London went more smoothly than I'd anticipated.

At least practically.

Jeff came through on his offer of a position in his company and was incredibly generous with his time as I settled into my new role there, first as a software engineer to learn the ropes and the products, then as a product manager heading up my own team.

While I'm still intending to set up and run my own business one day, this job is the perfect way to keep the money coming in for Mum's care whilst also giving me real-world business experience that I'll find incredibly helpful in the future.

My mum initially settled well into her new assisted-living home when we first got here, but as time went on, it became clear her health was deteriorating more rapidly than before. I'm trying not to think about how little time I might have left with her.

At least she's nearby and I can visit her on a regular basis, even though she's recognising me less and less frequently.

You've just got to keep moving forwards, right?

And considering how I've landed on my feet with this job, I should be satisfied with the way things have turned out. And I am. It's just that since leaving Bath, I've been left with a nagging feeling that I've walked away from something – or someone – really important.

And I don't mean Bea.

She and I have kept in touch and I've been relieved to hear she's getting on so well with her new career. It's not one I would have guessed she'd love like she does, but there you go. People surprise me all the time.

Information about how Dee's getting on is more of a black hole. I don't feel able to ask Bea about her and I'm not sure Dee would read a message from me without immediately deleting it after the way I behaved the last time we saw each other.

It was a little harsh of me – okay, very harsh – cutting her dead like I did the day we got back to Bath from our Greek adventure. But at that point, I had nothing left. I was exhausted, emotionally drained, worried – scared, even.

I hadn't wanted her to see that, though. Because if she had, she might have tried even harder to persuade me to do the thing I really wanted, but knew I didn't really have the option, to do.

Stay.

With her.

Instead, I pushed away what I wanted, got real and did the most practical thing I could.

And so here I am. In a much stronger position than I was four months ago.

Though considerably lonelier.

* * *

I'm coming out of the glass-fronted skyscraper near Aldgate Tube station in the City, where Blackmore Business Partners' headquarters are situated, thinking about what I'm going to eat for dinner tonight, when a movement and a flash of colour in my peripheral vision catches my attention and makes me slow my pace.

There's something about it that shoots a shiver of recognition straight down my spine.

'Hello, Numbers,' a voice says behind me.

I'd know that voice anywhere.

'Dee? What the hell are you doing here?' I say, turning to face her.

She looks good. More than good.

'What? Here in London? I didn't realise you'd bagsied the whole city,' she says, but with her usual playful grin lighting up her face.

It's impossible not to smile back at her.

'I meant here, outside my place of work.'

'You work here?' she teases, throwing her hands up in mock-surprise. 'Well, what a coincidence!'

Impossible not to laugh at that too.

It hits me that I haven't laughed in a very long while. Not properly. Not since I was last with Dee, in fact. Because, as I've come to realise, it's impossible not to find the fun in life when she's around.

'You've been waiting for me, haven't you,' I say, pretty sure that's the case.

'Yeah. You've got me there, MENSA Man.' She's still grinning at me, her eyes alive with mischief.

I assumed that after the way I left – particularly the last contact I had with her that day in Bea's flat – that I'd never hear from her again.

I guess that makes me an ass.

'So? Why are you here, waiting for me?' I ask her. Clearly, she's going to make me work for any sensible sort of information.

She gives a nonchalant shrug. 'Actually, I just thought I'd come and see what you gave up that lovely, dank basement office for.' Looking up at the monolith of a building that Jeff's filled with his expert workforce, she lets out a low whistle. 'Impressive gaff, Jem.'

'Thank you,' I say, supressing another smile.

'Anyway. I didn't mean to bother you,' she says, folding her arms and rocking back on her heels. 'I was in the area and thought I'd do a stroll-by. I didn't think I'd actually see you.'

I look at her for a beat, my heart thumping against my ribcage.

'Okay. Well, since you *have* seen me, do you fancy going for a quick drink to catch up? It'll be good to hear what you've been up to. I've been wondering.'

She blinks at me, shocked. 'Um. Err. Yeah? Sure. Okay. I could do that, I guess?'

'As long as I'm not inconveniencing you,' I say, raising an eyebrow at her apparent reluctance.

Is she regretting doing her stroll-by now?

There's a moment where she stares at me, her brows furrowed and her gaze piercing, then the expression in her eyes softens. 'You're not.'

We continue to look at each other for a few more beats and something profound passes between us.

Tacit understanding.

Something I've never experienced before with another living soul.

I feel like Dee just *gets* me.

I think she always has.

'Okay, let's go. There's a decent bar a couple of streets away,' I say, waving my hand in the general direction of it.

'Great,' Dee says.

* * *

Thankfully, it's pretty quiet in the pub I've chosen and we easily find a free table. I go to the bar for drinks while Dee settles herself onto a seat by the Edwardian etched-glass window that runs along one whole side of the pub.

When I return with the drinks, she takes hers from me with a nod of thanks and has a sip of it while I pull out a stool next to her and sit on it.

'So? How's life treating you?' I ask.

'Pretty good.'

'Yeah?'

'Yeah.'

'And? Is there more information forthcoming?'

She lets out a snort of amusement. 'You always did get straight to the point. I like that.'

'You know me, I'm an information guy.'

'So you are, Numbers. So you are.'

I wait for her to continue, watching with interest as she takes a big swig of her wine.

'Okay, so... as you probably know, I lost my job at the hotel and I needed to find something else to keep me afloat.'

'Yes?'

'And I figured it was a good opportunity to change the way I'd been thinking about how to get where I wanted to go.'

'Okay.'

'A friend of mine from college had just moved to London and let me sleep on her sofa for a couple of weeks while I looked for jobs, in exchange for me cleaning the flat and cooking all the evening meals.'

'Oh yeah?'

I take a swig of my beer, intrigued to know where this story is going. It's so good to see her, I'm feeling a rush of what I think must be endorphins. I certainly feel happier than I have in a long time.

'I knew I needed to do something new. Something different. Away from the comfort of my family.' Her eyes widen, like she's asking me for my understanding of the situation.

I nod.

'And I decided it was time I got my shit together and started looking after myself.'

'Uh-huh.'

'Because you were right.'

I blink at her, surprised by this admission. 'I was? About what?'

'About how selfish I was being, expecting other people – mostly Bea' – she holds up her hands in deferential recognition – 'to take care of me and fix the mess I was making of my life. It wasn't fair for me to expect her to do that.'

I nod again slowly. 'I see.'

'And I decided not to take the money from my dad, since I didn't really feel like I'd earned it. It would have been another easy route and I figured it was better to challenge myself and see if I could get by on my wits instead of his money.'

She runs a hand through her hair and her familiar scent hits my nose, sending my body into overdrive. I've missed the smell of her – as weird as it is to admit that. There's something so comforting and so thrilling about it.

'So I made a plan,' she continues, luckily oblivious to my mini-meltdown. 'One I stuck to, as best I could, and it seems to have paid off. I juggled a couple of different jobs for a while when I first moved here, working in a cocktail bar in Soho at night and a posh restaurant in Kensington during the day, and managed to scrape together a decent amount from my tips and pay. I've managed to land a new role recently though, which is really exciting. And I've worked on my paintings in every spare minute I've had. When my friend's flatmate moved out to go and live with her boyfriend, I took her room and scrimped and saved every penny I could. If I never eat another noodle in my life, it'll be too soon.' She grimaces.

'I can't lie, it's been bloody hard work,' she goes on, clearly on a roll now, 'but I'm proud of myself. I've not lost a job since the one at the hotel and everything I've landed since then has been on my own merit.'

'Impressive.'

I'm not bullshitting her either. I'm seriously impressed.

'Not really,' she says, the corner of her mouth lifting, as if she's taken my response as joshing. 'It's what everyone else does, right? I've just joined the real world.'

I can't help smiling back. 'And how are you finding that?'

'Exhausting, if I'm honest.' Lifting her hand, she yawns behind it. 'See?' she says, waving a finger towards her mouth to illustrate her point.

'So where are you working now?'

'Well, that's the cool bit. At Fenchurch Fine Art Gallery. I managed to talk the owner into giving me a shot there. I'm mostly doing the donkeywork of organising exhibitions and manning the desk when he's not around, but I'm enjoying it. There's a lot of face-to-face interactions, which I'm good at, and I feel like I'm learning the biz from the ground up. My background knowledge in art has been incredibly useful, plus the things I learnt to do at the hotel have ended up being a help too. You'll no doubt be surprised to know that I haven't been late for work once and I very much don't intend to be either. I'm taking this very seriously.' She picks up her drink and takes a big gulp, before smiling at me. It's a genuine smile, full of warmth.

My heart flips.

'That's great, Dee.'

'I've not told you the best bit yet.'

'Which is?'

'I met a couple of artists recently through the gallery and they invited me to exhibit some of my paintings at an event they were holding at their artists' collective studio, and I managed to sell four of them.'

She beams at me and I can't help but smile back.

'Congratulations.'

'Thank you,' she says, colour rising to her cheeks now. 'And off the back of it, I've got some space exhibiting at an artists' fair at Somerset House in a couple of months, which is ridiculously exciting. So keep your fingers crossed for me. It could make the world of difference to my career.'

I want to reach out and pull her into a hug, but I resist the urge. It feels like too much of a liberty right now. 'I'm happy for you, Dee. Seriously.'

'Thanks,' she says again, her eyes shining with pleasure.

The sight of it makes a bubble of joy rise in my chest.

'I figured, if I really wanted to be a career artist, I ought to stop fannying around, waiting for it to happen *to* me. That was never going to work.'

'Sounds sensible.'

'Well, you inspired me.'

I let out an involuntary snort. 'Really?'

'Yup.'

'Huh.'

'No need to sound so shocked. I do pay attention to the things people tell me sometimes. Especially people I respect.'

'Wow. That's not something I ever thought I'd hear come out of your mouth,' I tease.

'Well, I live to shock.' She winks at me. 'Especially you.'

My entire body responds to this, sending a rush of ecstatic energy through every muscle.

Dee doesn't seem to notice my sexual distraction, though.

'Honestly, I want to be the sort of person you respect, in the same way you respect Bea. And I guess I should thank you for being so honest with me and helping me realise that. I needed a boot up the arse.'

'Well, I'd like to say it was my pleasure, but I never took any pleasure in having a go at you. It was down to pure frustration,' I say, aware that my voice seems to have deepened by an entire octave.

'Yeah, I got that. You don't have a mean bone in your body, Numbers.'

'Thanks.'

'Though I know you definitely have another kind of bone, in certain situations...'

Jesus.

'Is this another one of your trouser-snake jokes?' I say, trying very hard not to remember all the times she's seen that particular bone. And, predictably, it decides to make another entrance at the memories. I'm very grateful that I'm sitting behind a table right now.

'You know me so well,' she says with a grin.

'Yeah. I guess I do.'

We look at each other while the meaning of that sinks in. Because we do know each other pretty well after spending that intense time together on Kapheira island. It irretrievably bonded us together, I think.

My pulse picks up its beat as I look into her deep blue eyes. She has such charismatic personality in her face, I can't help but gaze at it in wonder.

'So are you seeing anyone at the moment?' Dee asks, breaking into my distracted trance.

'I've been on a couple of dinner dates recently with a friend of a friend, but there wasn't any chemistry, so there's been no one serious, no.'

She nods.

'How about you?' I ask, preparing myself for a declaration about how in love she is with some incredible guy that I'm no doubt going to hate the sound of. Not that I want her to be unhappy. Just not happier without me.

'No one special,' she says, giving a shrug of her shoulder. 'Actually.' She huffs out a sigh. 'Honestly? I haven't dated since I last saw you. I've been too focused on getting my career back on track.'

I'm stunned. She's not dated for four months? 'Oh. Right,' is the only response I have. All other words have deserted me.

'I'm surprised half the population of London hasn't been throwing themselves at *your* feet, though,' she says with a grin, saving me from my awkwardness.

'Well, they may have been, but I've been pretty focused on other things, so too busy to notice,' I joke.

'How's your mum?' she asks, catching me off guard. 'Did the move to London go okay?'

I rub my hand over my brow, trying to soothe the sudden tension there. 'Uh, she's not great, to be honest. She barely recognises me any more when I visit and doesn't tend to engage in much going on around her. She's barely talking now. I feel like she's pretty much gone, at least in spirit.' Sadness coils in my gut.

'Oh, Jem, I'm so sorry,' Dee says with genuine empathy in her voice.

'Yeah. It sucks. She doesn't seem unhappy though, so that's a blessing at least. And I feel like she occasionally knows I'm there and that I love her and care about her, even if she's not sure who I am.'

Dee clears her throat. 'You know... if you like... I could come with you sometime when you visit her? For moral support? And I'd love to meet your mum.'

The idea of this sobers me up instantly. I'm not sure I want to cross those streams. As much as I appreciate the gesture, I feel like I want to keep the way I feel about each of them separate in my head.

'I'm not sure that's a good idea. It's confusing for her to meet new people,' I say.

But do I mean that? It might actually be good to have someone else there when I visit. Someone who understands me. Someone I don't have to pretend with.

'Okay, well, you know, if you change your mind, or ever want to talk to someone, or just go for a coffee sometime and *not* talk about it, then give me a call, okay? I'm around and I'd be happy to meet up. As friends,' she says.

She leans forwards, putting the flats of her hands onto the table, right by where I'm resting mine, but with enough space between them that they don't touch. Even so, my skin prickles with awareness.

'I know I'm no expert in grief, or dealing with something as traumatic as the things you've been through – and are still going through – but I'd like to help in any way I can,' she says with complete seriousness. 'Support you. If you'd like me to. And if you don't, then I'll understand and leave you alone. I just want what's best for you. Because I care about you.'

'Thanks.' I go to open my mouth and say more, but the words dry up in my mouth. I'm suddenly incredibly nervous and doubting everything I'm feeling. Am I reading this right? Does she just want to be friends with me now? And is that what I want? Do I actually want more? Can I have it?

Dee seems to take my uncommunicativeness as yet another rejection because she removes her hands from the table, then slaps them onto her knees and says, 'Okay, well, it's been good seeing you. I, err, have to go and meet a friend and I'm a bit late now. So, I guess I'll see you around.'

I watch her get up and start to put on her coat, a pulse beating hard in my temple.

I have a sudden urge to let her know I'm there for her too if she needs me and that I know she was there for Bea when it really mattered. I love that she stood up for her sister, even though it meant swallowing her pride and giving Bea centre stage once again.

Which must have been hard for her after striving for equal attention her whole life. She's been constantly forced to fight to get it – but never quite got there.

But she's still fighting for what she wants.

Her dad's indifference and her mum's jealousy could have broken her, but she's refused to let it.

You've got to respect that.

I do respect that.

And I'm coming to realise that that's exactly the kind of fighting spirit I want in a partner. Someone who doesn't give up.

But I need just a bit more time to think about this. I don't want to jump into it and get it wrong. Perhaps we should try being friends first.

'Dee?'

'Yeah?' She turns back to look at me, already a couple of steps away.

'Are you free for lunch on Saturday? There's a place near my flat that I've been meaning to check out, but I feel weird about going there on my own.'

'Oh! Well, sure. Yeah, I'd love to save you from an embarrassing situation. It's about time I made up for all the times I've caused them.' The grin she gives me is one of pure mischief.

There's a lifting sensation in my chest.

'Great. I'll message you.'

'Cool.'

19

DELILAH

It's only a couple of days before I hear from him, but it feels like another four months.

Because seeing Jem again cemented something for me. That I love him.

I'm completely *in* love with him, to be precise.

I think I probably always have been. I've just been too immature to fully realise it.

I feel like I've grown up a lot recently, though. I just wish I knew how to prove that to him.

Not that it would necessarily change anything for him in terms of how he feels about me.

Even after I told him about what I'd been doing for the last few months, he didn't seem to see it as anything special, from the way he reacted. Or, more to the point, *didn't* react.

But, I guess, judging it against most grown-up people's actions, it probably isn't that special.

It's leaps for me, though.

I'm proud of myself. And that's what really matters.

And if I only ever get to be friends with him, then so be it. I'll just have to accept that.

But if that *is* the case, I'm going to go down fighting – if you'll excuse the innuendo.

To that end, I find myself standing outside the door to Jem's flat in a 1930s red-brick mansion block in Marylebone at midday on Saturday, preparing myself for the worst, but hoping for the best.

Apparently, my brain appears to be too addled to think in anything other than comforting clichés right now.

I wait, with my heartbeat thumping in my ears, for him to open the door to me.

When he does, the sight of him literally takes my breath away. Seriously, I can barely drag a breath into my lungs, I'm suddenly so overwhelmed.

'Hey,' he says, giving me a strained-looking smile.

For one horrible moment, I wonder whether he's changed his mind about seeing me.

'Everything okay?' I ask, aware of a tremble in my voice.

Keep it together, Delilah.

'Yeah. Fine. I was just doing a bit of coding and forgot what time it was,' Jem says distractedly. 'Come in a sec.'

I nod and step into his flat, closing the door behind me.

Why am I feeling so disappointed? Did I really think he was going to bound up to the door and delightedly drag me inside and kiss me?

Only in my dreams, it seems.

I cross my arms and go to lean against the wall in the hall to wait for him as he disappears further into the flat.

'Actually, do you mind if I finish what I was doing?' he calls. 'It'll only take a couple of minutes. The place doesn't take bookings at lunchtime so we can go whenever we're ready.'

'Sure,' I say, though it's clear I don't actually have a say in this.

Kicking off my shoes and hanging my coat on a peg on the wall, I walk in the direction he disappeared and find myself in a living-kitchen-diner. Jem is sitting at the counter, tapping away on a laptop.

'Feel free to make yourself a cup of tea,' he says, not looking up from the screen.

I nod, which of course he doesn't see, then go to find mugs and teabags in his kitchen. I make two cups of tea and put one onto the counter next to him, then go and sit on a couch which is pushed up against the back wall, under a window that looks out over a park on the other side of the road.

I sip my tea and watch him as he works, finding I'm relieved to have a bit of time to pull myself together before I get his attention again. I don't want to spin out and make a mess of this and scare him off.

After another minute or two of furious typing, he finally shuts his laptop and picks up his tea, walking over to where I'm sitting and joining me on the couch. The cushion dips as he sits down and I shift my position so I can turn to look at him comfortably.

He looks back at me, his gaze searching mine. There's an unreadable expression on his face and it's making me nervous.

Huh. I thought he'd want to go out straight away, not sit here and chat.

'How was your week?' he asks, then takes a sip of tea.

'Fine. Nothing much to report,' I say. 'How about you?'

'Yeah. Fine,' he says. 'Busy.'

Okay, if we're just going to bat small talk back and forth, this could turn out to be excruciating. And I'm not having that.

I want the easy friendliness we had on the island back again. So much, it hurts.

So I decide just to dive straight in.

'Bea tells me you've been in regular touch with her. I think she really appreciates it. It's made it easier for her to forge ahead with what she really wants to do with her life.'

Jem seems a little taken aback at my segue into such a potentially controversial topic, but he recovers quickly and gives me a tight smile.

'Yeah, well, she's one of my best friends. I was never going to hold that against her. You've got to go with the flow sometimes, right? There's no point getting upset about something that was never meant to be.'

My heart starts to race as I consider asking him the thing that's been on my mind constantly for the last four months. I really want to know the answer, but then I also don't, especially if it's not what I want to hear.

But I have to. It's important I know where I stand, so I can get on with my life, one way or the other.

Better to get it over and done with now, while we're in the privacy of his flat, instead of in front of a bunch of strangers in a restaurant, I figure.

I take a breath, open my mouth, shut it, then give myself an internal shake and before I lose my nerve, I ask, 'Are you still in love with her?'

He looks at me for a beat and I stare back at him, trying to work out what the expression on his face means. Every nerve in my body is jumping in anticipation.

Finally, he shakes his head, frowns and says, 'No. I don't think I ever was. I idealised her, I think. But I put her so high on a pedestal, I couldn't touch her.'

Sweet relief rushes through me from the crown of my head to the tips of my toes.

I can't help the widest grin from breaking across my face. 'But you could touch me?'

He grins back. 'Yes. I very much wanted to touch you. A little too much, some might say, for someone who was set on not having a relationship at that point.'

I swallow past a tightness that's forming in my throat.

'I think the idea of loving Bea was safe because we were probably never going to actually get together, only in my imagination,' Jem says, seemingly unaware of how his confession is affecting me. 'Whereas you – you were danger personified. You made me feel things. Things I didn't want to feel. Things I couldn't put a name to. I was fascinated by you, but scared of you as well. I think, in my mind, you weren't a safe bet. I thought you'd get bored with someone as straight as me and leave. And I couldn't bear the idea of being left by another person I love. I know that probably sounds ridiculous, but after losing my dad so suddenly, then my mum so slowly, I'm scared of the idea of loving someone else in case I lose them too.'

I nod, still fighting with the tightness in my throat. 'That's not ridiculous. That's being human.'

'Yeah. I guess,' he says, giving me a sad smile that nearly breaks my heart.

'I know I put up a good front,' I say quietly, 'but I've never felt completely secure either, especially after my parents divorced. But before that too, because for as long as I can remember, they were always at each other's throats, each threatening to leave the other on a regular basis, in front of Bea and me too. I thought at one point, I'd be relieved if they split up, but when it actually happened, it changed everything, and not in a good way. It turned our whole lives upside down and pulled Bea and me further apart. So, I guess I've always felt a bit... lost and kind of alone, but I learnt how to pretend to everyone that it didn't bother me, when actually, it really, really did.'

'Yeah. I know exactly how that feels,' he says with such emotion in his voice, it stops me in my tracks.

And it suddenly hits me that *of course* he knows what that feels like. His parents relied on him to keep them all going for so long, he's never felt safe to show his real feelings either. Never felt that security that I crave too. He's always been alone, dealing with very serious things, being the adult in the room because no one else has been in good-enough health to do it.

Oh my God. How utterly naïve have I been about what he's had to go through? At least I've had Bea. He's had no one.

He still has no one.

My memory jumps back to his expression when he talked about how his mum doesn't recognise him any more, and my heart gives a painful throb.

It strikes me how his life and mine have been so very different. There's no wonder he's been so scathing of my behaviour in the past. He just saw me swanning around, flitting from one thing to the next, seemingly without a care in the world, when at the end of the day, he had to go and visit someone he loved who barely recognised him or acknowledged his presence.

It's been a long time since someone looked after *him*.

'Jem?'

'Yeah?'

'I need to tell you something.'

'Okay.'

'I love you.' I swallow past the lump forming in my throat and rush on, before I lose my nerve. 'I think about you all the time. And I miss you. So much, it physically hurts.' I tap my chest, over my heart. 'Right here. And I don't expect you to say that back to me,' I go on, before he has chance to reply. 'I know you've got more important things to worry about right now and I'm not your type and I'm, let's face it, a bit of a nightmare, but I just wanted to tell you that I think you're amazing and I'll always be there for you, even if it's just as a friend – if that's what you want. I don't want you to be lonely any more. It breaks my heart to think that you are.'

I'm aware that my hand holding my cup of tea is shaking and slopping tea onto my lap. Jem notices too, because he takes the cup from me and turns to put it onto the table next to him, along with his own.

He turns back to face me and I fully expect to see a look of either frustration or regret on his face.

But there's not a trace of either emotion.

Instead, his eyes seem to be shining with a mixture of understanding and... burning need.

Before I know what's happening, he's kissing me full on the mouth, sliding his hand round to cradle the back of my neck and hold me tightly, as if he's determined to keep me there until he's done what he needs to do.

But I'm not going anywhere.

My heart is fluttering hard in my chest and the whole of my skin feels electrified in the most energising, sensational way.

I'm in heaven.

I kiss him back, opening my mouth to give him full access, and I dart my tongue against his, rejoicing in the long-missed taste of him.

He releases his hold on my neck and moves his hands slowly down my body, exploring the dips and curves of my throat, then lower, his fingers roving over the swells of my breasts, immediately making my nipples stand to attention. It's as if he's reacquainting himself with them after too long away.

I moan my pleasure into his mouth, hoping he'll move lower still, needing his touch so desperately, I'm half wild with it.

He leans into me, pushing me back onto the sofa so he can

press his body urgently into mine, from hip to chest, and rock against me, causing the most delicious friction between us. Clearly, he's just as turned on by this as I am.

'Dee?' he says in an urgent tone.

'Yeah,' I breathe against his mouth.

'I really want to make love to you.'

My grin is so wide, my cheeks ache. Make love. That's so adorable. And so hot.

'I want my first time to be with you,' he says. 'It would mean everything to me.' He strokes his thumb across my cheek. 'Because I love you too.'

Oh my God, this is really happening. Jem loves me. I finally get to have him. It's like a dream coming true.

'I want that too,' I say in a rush of breath, my voice infused with the joy I'm feeling.

'Let's go to my bedroom. I have condoms in there,' he mutters, looking into my eyes to check I'm really happy to do this right now.

I nod enthusiastically, my heart beating in my throat. Because I am. This feels like exactly the right time.

In fact, I'm so excited about the idea, I can barely wait for him to move off me so I can dash into the bedroom and get right into it.

I hear him laugh behind me as I practically jump off the sofa and head out of the room, only to skid to a halt in the corridor, trying to decide whether the door to the left or the right is his bedroom.

'Turn right,' he says, directly behind me.

I grab the handle of the door and push it open, then run to his bed and throw myself onto it. It smells of him, all musky and minty and delicious, and I drag the scent in through my nose and deep into my lungs, feeling like I've just come home.

Jem rummages through one of the drawers in his bedside table and retrieves a condom then jumps onto the bed next to me, leaning in to kiss me hard again.

I don't think we've ever removed our clothes so quickly.

And then he's kneeling between my legs and rolling on the condom, looking down at me with such hunger, I feel the effects of it all the way through my body.

'Come here,' I say, motioning for him to lean in and kiss me again.

He complies, crushing my lips with his and sliding his tongue deep into my mouth.

We urgently touch each other's body all over, relearning what we used to know so well. He's so familiar and so utterly new and exciting at the same time, it gives me shivers of pleasure.

'Want me to make you come first?' he asks in a deep, gravelly sounding voice, like his lust has infused every part of him.

'No. I just want to feel you inside me. Now. I'm so ready already. I don't want to wait,' I say, my tone almost begging.

Honestly, I would absolutely beg for it right now if he asked me to. That would actually be pretty hot.

But he doesn't. He seems to be right there with me already and I suck in a breath of pure excitement as I feel the head of his cock pressing against the entrance to my pussy.

Slowly and oh so carefully, he pushes into me.

The delicious stretch as I accommodate the substantial girth of him is electrifying. It's even more satisfying than I imagined and I almost come from the feeling of it, tendrils of lust reaching deep inside me, making my whole body hum.

'Ohhh, that feels so good. So amazingly good,' I moan as he pushes deeper.

He stills above me, pressing his forehead to mine. 'Jesus, Dee. I told myself I wasn't going to do this. I thought we should spend some time together as friends first, at least. And see what developed.' Lifting his head, he pulls his hips back a little, pulling almost all the way out, then slides into me again. 'Slowly,' he says, torturing me as he stops his thrust just short of the deepest place inside me.

I wriggle beneath him, urging him to move again. *I want more, dammit!*

'But I just can't help myself around you,' he says with a smile in his voice.

'Good. I'm glad you can't. Because this is exactly what I wanted to happen,' I pant.

'Yeah?'

'Yeah.' The word comes out as a moan of pleasure as he thrusts inside me again.

'I've thought a lot about what it would be like to finally do this with you,' he mutters, his breath coming faster now.

'And?' I murmur back.

'It feels fucking fantastic.' He sucks in a breath as he moves into me again. 'A bit too good, if I'm honest,' he says with a strain in his voice now. 'I'm really close. Perhaps we should stop?'

'Don't you dare!' I wrap my arms around his back, preventing him from drawing away from me.

'You sure? What about you?'

'Don't worry about me. I want you to come. Whenever you're ready.'

'I'm so ready.'

'Do it. I want to feel you come inside me,' I demand. 'We'll do me later.'

This is all I've thought about in the last few days, finally feeling him fucking me. Just the thought of it has got me off more times than I'd like to admit. So I can wait for my orgasm.

I see him nod and he starts to thrust again, sliding into me over and over, getting deeper each time as he starts to lose his mind and stop worrying about how I'm feeling, now I've given him permission to.

I cling on to him, riding his thrusts, loving the sensation of him hitting so deep, lighting up all my nerve endings and making my entire body rush with the joy of it.

He's starting to shake now, clearly trying to hold on longer. I'm impressed he's made it this long, with it being his first time.

The thought of that sends another wave of pleasure rippling through me. It's almost akin to an orgasm in itself.

But he's clearly reached his limit of holding back and he begins to let out a low, growly sounding moan from deep within his throat and a few thrusts later, he finally lets go and shudders into his orgasm, pressing his body deep into mine.

It's the hottest thing *ever*.

I run my hands over the warm skin of his back as he tries to get his breathing under control again, feeling the sheen of sweat he's worked up coat my fingertips.

Also so *very* hot.

'Are you okay?' I ask, smiling at the way he's gone all floppy with relief above me.

'Hell yes,' he says, his voice muffled against my hair.

After another few moments of getting his head together, he finally rolls away from me, disposes of the condom, then pulls me against the side of his body, wrapping his arms around me.

'Are *you* okay?' he asks.

'Oh yes.'

'Just give me a second and I'll be right back with you,' he says with a grin in his voice.

'No rush,' I say, running my fingers over the swell of his bicep. 'I've got all day.'

'I'm so glad you came over,' he says, pulling me close to kiss my forehead, before letting me go again.

I tip my head and wrinkle my nose at him. 'You know, I really thought you were going to tell me you didn't want to be more than friends after the way you greeted me at the door.'

He rubs his hand over his face, then peeks out at me from between his fingers. 'I'm sorry about that. I've been on edge all morning about seeing you and when you knocked on the door, I kind of freaked out.'

'So you weren't working?'

He lets out a huff of amusement and uncovers his face, looking me fully in the eye. 'No. I was just typing nonsense onto a document while I tried to get my shit together. I needed a moment to... I don't know what. I had no idea how to act when I saw you.'

'Me neither.'

'I guess we were just kidding ourselves. There was no way we weren't going to end up like this.'

'Honestly, I really hoped we would. Prayed for it, in fact.'

He smiles and leans in to kiss me.

Reaching up, I run my hands from his collarbones to his hips, a wide smile breaking out across my face.

'What are you grinning about?' he asks with a quizzical twist to his mouth.

'The fact I've well and truly de-virginised you now.'

'Is that even a word?' he asks sceptically, adding his trademark eyebrow raise.

Oh, how I've missed that expression.

'It is now. I've coined it. You heard it here first. Mark this moment and alert the dictionary people.'

He laughs, deep in his throat.

It's the best sound in the world.

'Thank you for letting it be me that had that pleasure,' I say.

'It was *my* pleasure.'

I raise my own eyebrow at him. 'You know, before we met up the other day and you told me you'd not dated since we last saw each other, I was really jealous at the thought of you losing your virginity to someone else.'

'Jealous? Really?'

'Yeah. I've thought about it a lot, actually.'

'When you were wanking?' he asks with a twinkle in his eye.

I grin at him. 'Got it in one.'

Lifting his hand, he smooths my hair down, sending more shivers of pleasure through me. I feel so looked after. So seen.

'You know, I didn't tell you this in the pub for fear of sounding patronising, but I'm blown away by how you've managed to get your shit together. How hard you've worked for it. It's seriously impressive. I'm in awe.'

Warmth rushes to my cheeks at his compliment. 'Yeah, well, I had to prove you wrong. It was a strong driving factor. I wanted to *finally* impress you.'

'Well, you did.'

He leans forward and kisses me lightly on the lips. 'And since we're spilling our guts, I wanted to tell you that you were right.'

'About what?'

'About me needing you. To help me find the fun. That time we spent on the island was the best week of my life. I've never laughed so much. And I miss it. I've missed *you*. So much.'

'I've missed you too, Numbers.'

We grin at each other like loons for a moment.

'So, should we go for that meal soon?' I ask, starting to explore the toned plains of his body with my fingertips again, hoping he's going to say he doesn't feel like doing that any more. I know I don't. I'd happily stay here in bed with him for the rest of the day and feast on him instead.

He turns to look at me, staring deep into my eyes, as if he's looking for my true thoughts on the matter. I stare back, willing him to read my mind. Fascinated to know if he can actually intuit how I'm feeling as well as I hope he can.

'Nah,' he says. 'You're the only thing I want to eat right now.'

I let out a loud, delighted laugh. 'Thank God for that!' I say as he rolls on top of me and kisses me hard. I feel his body respond to me immediately and smile against his mouth.

Drawing away from me, he gently brushes a strand of hair away from my face. It's the most loving, caring gesture ever and my heart gives a swoop of joy as I take in the exultant expression on his face.

He stares into my eyes for what seems like eons, while whole silent conversations pass between us.

'I'm going to make you so happy,' he says confidently, his mouth crooking into a smile.

I smile back. 'You don't need to. I already am.'

'Good,' he says, 'I want that for you.' He cups my face with his hands. 'Because I love you,' he murmurs, his gaze firmly locked with mine.

Then he kisses me deeply again and proceeds to show me just how much he means it.

* * *

MORE FROM CHRISTY McKELLEN

Another book from Christy McKellen, *Best Laid Plans*, is available to order now here:

https://mybook.to/BestLaidPlansBackAd

ACKNOWLEDGEMENTS

Huge thanks, as ever, to the amazing Boldwood team – especially my wonderful editor Megan. I'm also so grateful to Niamh for her ninja marketing skills and tireless efforts to get my stories into readers' hands. A big thank you to both copyeditor Emily and proofreader Jennifer for catching my clangers! I'm incredibly lucky to have the very talented Leah Jacobs-Gordon designing my stunning covers – they never fail to make me gasp with delight when I first get to see them, so thank you, Leah. Lastly, thanks to you, reader, for choosing and reading my stories.

ABOUT THE AUTHOR

Christy McKellen is the author of provocative and sexy romance novels that have sold over half a million copies worldwide.

If you enjoyed this book, sign up to Christy McKellen's newsletter to get the ebook of her spicy romance *Hearts on Ice* for FREE!

Visit Christy's website: www.christymckellen.com

Follow Christy on social media here:

- facebook.com/christymckellenauthor
- x.com/ChristyMcKellen
- instagram.com/christymckellen
- bookbub.com/authors/christy-mckellen

ALSO BY CHRISTY MCKELLEN

Three's a Crowd

Marry Me...Maybe?

About Last Night

Best Mistake Ever

Here Comes Trouble

So That Happened

The Paradise Hook-Up

Boldwood

EVER AFTER

x♡x♡

JOIN BOLDWOOD'S
**ROMANCE
COMMUNITY**
FOR SWEET AND
SPICY BOOK RECS
WITH ALL YOUR
FAVOURITE
TROPES!

SIGN UP TO OUR
NEWSLETTER

HTTPS://BIT.LY/BOLDWOODEVERAFTER

Boldw‍ood

Boldwood Books is an award-winning fiction
publishing company seeking out the best
stories from around the world.

Find out more at www.boldwoodbooks.com

Join our reader community for brilliant books,
competitions and offers!

Follow us
@BoldwoodBooks
@TheBoldBookClub

Sign up to our weekly
deals newsletter

https://bit.ly/BoldwoodBNewsletter